THE DRAGON'S EGG

ALISON BAIRD

Illustrations by Frances Tyrrell

Cover by Daniel Potvin

Scholastic Canada Ltd.

Toronto New York London Auckland Sydney
Mexico City New Delhi Hong Kong Buenos Aires

Scholastic Canada Ltd.
604 King Street West, Toronto, Ontario M5V 1E1, Canada

Scholastic Inc.
557 Broadway, New York, NY 10012, USA

Scholastic Australia Pty Limited
PO Box 579, Gosford, NSW 2250, Australia

Scholastic New Zealand Limited
Private Bag 94407, Botany, Manukau 2163, New Zealand

Scholastic Children's Books
Euston House, 24 Eversholt Street, London NW1 1DB, UK

www.scholastic.ca

Library and Archives Canada Cataloguing in Publication
Baird, Alison, 1963-
The dragon's egg / by Alison Baird ; interior illustrations by
Frances Tyrrell ; cover illustration by Daniel Potvin.
ISBN 978-1-4431-2444-7
I. Tyrrell, Frances, 1959- II. Title.
PS8553.A367D73 2013   jC813'.54   C2012-907800-X

6 5 4 3 2 1   Printed in Canada 121   13 14 15 16 17

MIX
Paper from
responsible sources
FSC
www.fsc.org   FSC® C004071

Contents

For my parents.
A.B.

Chapter one

Ai Lien

Ai Lien Feng ran home through the sunny September afternoon, full of excitement. She was running because it was her birthday, and because her parents would be home from work early to help her celebrate it. She could hardly wait to get there.

Home was a small house in downtown Toronto, which she shared only with her father and mother. She had no brothers or sisters; there was only her grandmother, who lived in her own home next door. The Feng family was Chinese, though only Mr. Feng and his mother had actually lived in China. Ai Lien and her mother had both been born in Canada.

Mr. Feng often talked fondly of China to his daughter.

He had several big beautiful books filled with photographs that Ai Lien liked to pore over on rainy days, gazing at the oddly shaped green mountains, curly roofed pagodas, and boats called junks with their sails that looked like half-opened fans. Mr. Feng had promised to take her to China someday, when he went on one of his business trips. He had just been there recently, Ai Lien knew, and she had a feeling that at least one of the presents waiting for her had been brought from that faraway land.

It was her ninth birthday, and this year the presents were especially nice: there was a new doll from her grandmother, some interesting-looking books from her mother, and an embroidered robe with a pair of matching slippers, which her father had, indeed, brought all the way from China. He had brought her something else, too: a smooth grey stone, which he had picked up on the bank of the Yangtze River when he went there on a boat tour.

"A little piece of China for you to keep," he told her as he put the stone in her hand. Then he leaned close and added in a low voice: "There's something special about that stone. It looked just the same as all the other stones, but when I picked it up in my hand it had a strange *feel* to it — something magical. I wouldn't be a bit surprised if it turned out to be a dragon's egg!"

"A dragon's egg!" Ai Lien repeated.

He nodded, his eyes twinkling. "You remember I told you about Chinese dragons, how very different they are from the dragons of the West. They don't breathe fire or eat people. Chinese dragons are very civilized. They can talk, and cast magic spells and change their shapes whenever they want to. They don't live in caves but in beautiful palaces at the bottoms of rivers, where they rule over all the fish and water-creatures. And when these clever dragons lay their eggs on the river bank they disguise them as stones, to protect them from anyone who might find them."

Ai Lien thought that was a lovely idea. When she went up to bed that night she placed the stone reverently on her dresser, next to her bowl of goldfish. She had three goldfish, named Pearl, Jade and Plum Blossom, and she was extremely proud of them. Her father had told her that it was the Chinese who invented goldfish, breeding them from much bigger fish called carp. Ai Lien's fish were very beautiful, with long delicate fins and scales that gleamed like gold coins. She gave them their food, said good night to them, and got into bed, turning out the light.

She was awakened in the night by a noise.

Opening her eyes, she saw that the sky outside was flickering with brilliant blue-white lightning. Thunder crashed and boomed overhead, but oddly there was no rain. And Ai Lien couldn't help feeling that it wasn't the thunder that had awakened her, but something else; a cracking, splintering noise, as if something in her bedroom had fallen and smashed on the floor. She sat up in bed and turned on the light, rubbing her eyes. Outside the thunder rumbled, more softly this time, then faded away. There was no more lightning. The house was very quiet: her clock said a quarter to twelve. What could have made that noise?

Then she saw that the stone her father had given her had fallen to the floor and broken into a dozen pieces. At once she jumped out of bed and picked up the broken bits. Her precious stone, that Daddy had brought her all the way from China! What could have happened to it? She turned the pieces over in her hands, seeing from the shape of them that the stone must have been hollow inside. And, strangely, the pieces were *wet*.

At that moment she heard something — a strange scurrying sound on the other side of the dresser. It sounded like something alive — a mouse, perhaps? Ai Lien went over to investigate.

The little animal she saw huddled on the floor was not

a mouse. It looked more like a little snake, though still unlike any snake that Ai Lien had ever seen. Its scales were red and golden, it had a green fringe around its neck like a mane, and there were two little knobs on its head, like the buds of horns. Ai Lien wasn't afraid of animals, even the ones that make some people shiver, like snakes and toads. She went right up to the little creature, gazing at it curiously; and then suddenly she realized what it was, and cried out in amazement and delight.

"A dragon! So it really *was* a dragon's egg!"

The baby dragon was startled. It had been blinking in the sudden light, and now when it heard Ai Lien's shout it slithered underneath the dresser. Seeing that it was frightened, Ai Lien spoke to it in a gentle voice.

"Come out, little dragon!" she called softly. "I won't hurt you!"

The tiny creature looked out from under the dresser, decided that she meant what she said, and came out again. Ai Lien bent down and picked it up, very gently.

"I'll put you into my goldfish bowl for the night. Dragons like the water, don't they? And I know you won't eat up my fish — Daddy said that dragons are related to carp, just like goldfish. I'm sure you wouldn't eat your own cousins!"

Ai Lien bent down and picked it up, very gently.

The little dragon liked the goldfish bowl. He swam around it several times and then settled down on the bottom, looking perfectly content. The goldfish didn't seem to mind sharing their bowl with him, either.

"Won't Daddy be thrilled that it was a dragon's egg!" said Ai Lien to herself. "I can't wait to tell him!" She thought of going and waking up her parents, but decided against it. They both worked so hard, they needed their sleep, and anyway the dragon would still be there in the morning. But it was hard to get back to sleep herself. She tossed and turned with excitement, and kept switching the light on to make sure it hadn't all been a dream. And each time the baby dragon was still there.

"Good night, dragon," she said finally, before turning out the light for the very last time. "I'll see you in the morning!"

And the little dragon lifted his head and looked at her, just as though he understood.

Chapter two

Lung Wang

When Ai Lien woke the next morning she had a happy, excited feeling inside, the sort of feeling that means the day to come is special in some way.

"But my birthday was yesterday," said Ai Lien to herself. "So it isn't that." Then she remembered the strange, wonderful dream she'd had last night — about a dragon hatching out of the stone her father had given her.

"I've never had a dream like that before," she yawned. "It seemed so real!" She sat up in bed, stretching — and then she sat very still, staring at her dresser. On it were the bits and pieces of the broken stone, where she'd put them the night before.

Well, she thought, *that part of it was real, anyway.* She looked at the goldfish bowl. The morning sun was streaming through it, so that the fish in it shone as if they were really made of gold.

And there was the baby dragon! He was floating at the surface with just his eyes and nose above the water, like a tiny alligator. His eyes were green as jade, and they looked into hers with a very intelligent expression.

Ai Lien jumped out of bed at once and ran downstairs without stopping to get dressed. Her father and mother were having breakfast at the kitchen table and she ran up to them excitedly.

"Daddy!" she cried, tugging at his sleeve. "You'll never guess — the most wonderful thing has happened! That stone you gave me really *was* a dragon's egg — it hatched last night!"

Mr. Feng put down his morning paper and smiled at his daughter. "Did it really?"

"The dragon's red and gold, with a green mane," went on Ai Lien. "And he's got green eyes."

"Has he indeed!" said her father.

He doesn't believe me, Ai Lien thought. Well, who could blame him? Laughing, she grabbed his hand and cried, "Come and see for yourself!"

"Ai Lien, dear, your father hasn't finished his

breakfast," said Mrs. Feng.

"Breakfast can wait," said Mr. Feng. "It isn't every day a dragon hatches in this house. Yes, Ai Lien, I'm coming."

Ai Lien practically flew up the staircase, so eager was she to show the dragon to her father. When he caught up with her at the top of the stairs she flung open her bedroom door, and cried dramatically, "Look!"

"Good heavens!" her father exclaimed in a tone of the utmost astonishment. "It's a dragon all right! Red and gold, with green eyes!"

Ai Lien was staring at the fish-bowl. There was nothing in it but goldfish, swimming to and fro.

"No, no, Daddy!" she cried. "It isn't a *pretend* dragon! He was real — he was here a moment ago — oh, where can he be?" She began to search through her room, pulling out the dresser drawers and hunting through the closet.

Mr. Feng glanced at his watch. "Well, I'll have to see the dragon after work," he said. "I've got to hurry now, or I'll be late. Have a good day, Ai Lien." He patted her shoulder and went back downstairs.

Ai Lien sat down slowly on her bed. She couldn't understand what had happened. "But the dragon was there," she kept saying to herself. "I saw it. It was *there*."

At last her mother had to call up the stairs to her, telling her to hurry up or she'd be late for school. She got dressed and ate breakfast and left the house, all as though she were in a trance.

When Ai Lien arrived at school the bell had rung and the playground was deserted, but that wasn't unusual for her. She had begun to make a habit of arriving at this time, not too late for the start of class but late enough so that she missed the time before the bell, when all the children gathered in the schoolyard. Ai Lien hated having to stand all by herself, watching them talking and laughing together. They never asked her to join them.

Her problems had begun on her first day here. She had done so well at school the year before that she had been moved ahead a whole grade, leaving her old classmates behind and going on to this new place, Thornwood Public School. At first she had been rather excited at the thought of going to a new school, but she soon began to find it depressing. She missed her old classmates, and she thought Thornwood was an ugly place, all asphalt and concrete, surrounded by chain-link fences. There was only one attractive part of the school grounds, a little narrow stretch of pine trees at the east end of the soccer field.

On her first day she recognized some other girls from

her last school standing near the entrance. She didn't know them well since they'd been in the grade ahead of her, but she knew their names: Mei, Patti and Sue. She went up to them, feeling a little shy, hoping to make friends.

"Hi," she said. "My name's Ai Lien — do you remember me, from Brookdale School? This is a much bigger place, isn't it? There's a nice little wood over there — why don't we go there and play tag, or something?"

The other girls stared at her. "Tag?" Patti repeated. "We're in Grade *Five* now, Ai Lien — we don't play games like the little kids any more."

"You played them last year," said Ai Lien, puzzled. "I saw you, in the playground."

"Oh, *last* year," said Mei. "We were fourth graders, it was okay to run around *then*."

"What do we do then, if we don't play any more?" Ai Lien asked.

"Stand around, and talk about stuff," Sue told her. "You know — boys, and TV, stuff like that." Ai Lien thought this sounded rather boring, and was about to say so frankly when she caught sight of a little gold earring shining in Patti's ear.

"You've got pierced ears!" she exclaimed in surprise.

"Of *course* they're pierced," returned Patti impatiently.

"We all had them done over the summer. When are you going to pierce yours?"

"And why do you wear such dumb clothes?" put in Mei. "Nobody wears *dresses* in Grade Five. We all wear jeans now. And shoes like these ones — " she held her own foot out "— especially this brand, they're the best. Tell your mom to buy you some."

"But why wear running shoes if you never run any more?" asked Ai Lien. It was all very confusing. She was beginning to wonder if perhaps she should have stayed in her own grade.

Mei was about to reply scornfully to this when a shout from behind made them all turn around. A large, freckle-faced boy stood there, scowling. "You girls — where's your ten cents?"

"Ten cents?" echoed Ai Lien, as the others rummaged quickly in their pockets. "What's that for?"

The boy grinned at her — a grin as ugly as his scowl. "For protection."

"Protection? From what?"

"From me." The grin stretched wider. "I'm Jake Bradley — heard of me? No? Well, you pay, see, or I beat you up. Got it?"

"No," answered Ai Lien. "I don't get it. Why should you beat me up?"

Jake glared at her. "Are you stupid or what? Who are you, anyway?" He peered at the flap of her school bag, where her name was printed in big block letters. "Alien? What kinda name is that? Is that what you are? An alien from outer space?" He looked at the other girls and they tittered nervously. "Hey, *Alien!*"

"Don't call me that!" cried Ai Lien. "I don't like it!"

Jake stared at her in disbelief. This little shrimp of a girl, daring to answer *him* back like that! He put his freckled face very close to Ai Lien's, so that she backed away, startled. "You pay," he said, breathing heavily. "Or else." Then he turned and stalked away.

Ai Lien watched him, shaken. No one had ever threatened her in her life, and she couldn't quite take it in. "I don't believe he beats anyone up," she said aloud, to reassure herself. "The teachers wouldn't let him."

"The teachers can't do anything about it," Patti told her. "Jake gets you when you're *off* school property. You shouldn't have talked to him like that, Ai Lien. I know a girl who went to Jake Bradley's school last year, and she told me it's not a good idea to get on his bad side. He's tough and really mean, so you'd better do as he says."

"I don't care!" Ai Lien burst out. "I don't care how mean he is, I'm not giving him any money!"

Then the girls all turned and moved off in a tight little group, leaving Ai Lien standing alone on the pavement. And since then, none of the other kids would have anything to do with her. If she tried to join the other girls in the school yard they would walk away. Jake and the group of boys who hung around with him did all they could to make her life miserable, throwing spitballs at her in class when the teacher wasn't looking, and pestering her as she stood all alone at recess.

Today as she sat in her seat at the back of the classroom Ai Lien's mind was far away. The teacher, Mrs. Jenkins, had to ask her the same question three times before she heard. Jake Bradley laughed out loud.

"Hey, Alien's spaced out!" he shouted, making the class titter while Ai Lien looked at the floor, close to tears. How could the dragon have been only a dream, when she'd seen him the next morning, plain as anything? But if he had been real — and she so wanted him to be — where had he gone?

Finally, during science, when Mrs. Jenkins was explaining about the different kinds of animals, Ai Lien put up her hand hesitantly.

"Yes, Ai Lien?" said the teacher.

"Please," she said, "are there — *could* there be — such things as dragons?"

The whole class shouted with laughter, until Ai Lien wanted to sink right through the floor with embarrassment. Everywhere she looked she saw pointing fingers and jeering mouths.

"Are there such things as dragons!" Jake roared, grinning around at the rest of the class. "What a stupid question!"

Fortunately science was the last class of the day, so Ai Lien could pull on her coat immediately afterwards and run home. Once the front door of the house had closed behind her she raced upstairs and flung herself down on her bed to bury her face in the pillow and let all the misery of the day sob itself out. There was no one to talk to but her old grandmother, who always came over from next door to stay with her after school until her parents came home. Grandmother was getting rather deaf and knew very little English. Mr. Feng was teaching Ai Lien Mandarin, but she could speak only a few words, so she and Grandmother didn't have much to say to each other. In any case, Grandmother had dozed off on the sofa downstairs, and the house was dark and still. Ai Lien felt very alone.

After a while she sat up and looked miserably at the

bowl on the dresser with its circling goldfish. *I really must have dreamed it after all,* she thought. *Dragons aren't real.*

Suddenly she noticed something very odd. She had only three fish, she knew. But now there were *four* swimming around in the bowl!

As she sat there staring, the fourth fish began to glow with a soft yellow light, changing its shape. And there, in its place, was the little dragon!

"Oh!" she gasped, leaping to her feet. "You were there all along!" And now she remembered what her father had told her about dragons being able to change their shapes. "Can you talk too?" she whispered. "Can you?"

"Of course I can talk," replied the creature in a high, piping voice, raising its head out of the water. "I am a dragon. Have you humans forgotten so much about us already?" It sounded rather indignant.

Ai Lien sat down again on her bed, feeling dizzy. "But — this is *wonderful!*" she gasped. Then a thought occurred to her. "But — *how* can you talk? I mean — if you hatched last night, you must be only a baby still."

"Of course, you're human," remarked the dragon with a superior air, "and human beings learn and grow very slowly. It's different with us dragons, because we are divine."

"What does 'divine' mean?" asked Ai Lien.

"It means magical — the very highest kind of magic there is, the magic of gods and spirits," replied the dragon. It left the bowl and slithered down onto the dresser. "My parents talked to me when I was still in the egg, and told me all I needed to know. And I've heard you and your father talking, of course — and those people in the magic mirror."

"Magic mirror?" repeated Ai Lien.

"That enchanted device the venerable lady was watching downstairs, which shows all that is happening in the world. The Yellow Emperor himself had nothing to compare with it! You must be powerful sorcerers."

"Oh, you mean the TV!" said Ai Lien. "It isn't magic really, it works by electricity."

"Electricity?"

"Yes — a sort of bluey light, like lightning, that runs along wires and makes things work."

"What!" exclaimed the little dragon, rearing its head high in amazement. "You control the power of lightning, like a dragon? You *must* be sorcerers, then!"

"No, really we're not. Everyone uses electricity. But you — can you really do magic?"

"Of course I can," said the dragon. "All dragons can do magic. We have power over the weather, the wind and the rain — that's why there's always a thunderstorm when one of us hatches, as no doubt you noticed. In the olden days your ancestors would pray to mine to make rain fall on their crops, or to send flooded rivers back to their beds. We also have power over all the creatures of the waters. Look!" The dragon turned toward the fish-bowl and uttered a curious musical sound.

All at once the goldfish in the bowl began to dance. Lifting their heads toward the water's surface, beating their fins rapidly, they began to spin around in a circle, their long tails swaying like ladies' skirts. Around and around they went, faster and faster; then they all leaped into the air, turning somersaults, and plopped back into the bowl.

"That was amazing!" cried Ai Lien, her eyes shining.

"Of course it was," answered the dragon smugly. "Dragons are amazing creatures. And I'm no ordinary dragon, either! I'm the son of the Dragon King of the Yangtze River."

"I didn't know dragons had kings," said Ai Lien, fascinated.

"Of course we have kings," said the dragon. "That's what my name means, you know — *Lung Wang* — Dragon King, because when I'm older I'll have a river-kingdom of my own. My father lives in a magnificent

. . . then they all leaped into the air, turning somersaults . . .

palace at the bottom of the Yangtze — at least I've heard it's magnificent. I haven't actually seen it, of course. I'll have to go back there someday, but I can't right now, as my *chi'h muh* hasn't grown yet."

"Your what?"

"My *chi'h muh* — a sort of scaly lump on my forehead that will enable me to fly through the air. Dragons, you know, are too magical to fly in the ordinary way, with wings. I will have legs though, when I've grown a bit more."

"You're like a tadpole then, that grows legs and turns into a frog," said Ai Lien, remembering her science classes.

"I am nothing at all like a frog," said Lung Wang with an injured air.

"Of course you aren't," Ai Lien soothed, seeing that the dragon's pride was hurt. "You're much more interesting! Oh, Lung Wang, won't you stay here with me? I'll look after you until you can fly back home to China."

"I would be delighted to stay with you — " Lung Wang paused, and looked at Ai Lien with a question in his eyes. "Ai Lien," she supplied quickly.

"Ai Lien," Lung Wang continued with an approving nod. "You seem a most sagacious person."

"What does 'sagacious' mean?" she asked.

"It means wise and full of insight — or so my father told me."

Ai Lien leaped up, unable to contain her joy and excitement any longer. It hadn't been a dream — the stone egg really had hatched, the dragon really was there. Now it was her unhappy day at school that seemed to her like a dream, a bad dream that was fast fading away. "What fun this is!" she said delightedly. "Everyone will love meeting you! My grandmother's downstairs right now, I'll go and wake her up — "

"No, no! You mustn't tell anyone about me!"

Lung Wang sounded so alarmed that Ai Lien stopped dancing about and stared at him in surprise. "But why not?"

"We dragons haven't mingled with you humans for hundreds of years. We prefer to keep our distance, now that you've grown so out of touch with the world of magic. That is why we learned to disguise ourselves. If your parents and grandmother see me, they'll want to rush out and tell all the other humans about me. They might even put me on the mirror-thing, for everyone to see! No, it wouldn't do at all. I can't help your having seen me, but nobody else must know."

Ai Lien wasn't too happy about this. She had so

wanted to tell her parents about the dragon. But the little creature seemed very anxious about it, so she promised not to tell anyone.

"Good, good," said Lung Wang, much relieved. "By the way, have you any food here? I'm ravenous, and goldfish food isn't particularly fortifying."

Ai Lien ran downstairs to the refrigerator, found some left-over fried pork and hurried upstairs with it. Her heart was pounding with excitement; she was half-afraid that Lung Wang would have vanished again when she got back to her room. But he was still there, eagerly waiting for his food. He snapped up the pork pieces in a matter of seconds.

"That's much better," he sighed. "I can feel myself growing already."

Just then they heard the front door open and Mr. Feng's voice called out, "Hello, I'm home!"

At once Lung Wang slithered over to the goldfish bowl and dropped into the water. In a moment there was nothing to be seen but another goldfish, swimming around in circles.

"Hello," said Mr. Feng, looking into the room. "Sorry I had to rush off this morning. . . . That's odd. There seem to be more fish than usual in your bowl. Did you buy another one?"

Ai Lien hesitated. "Uh — yes, I did."

"That's all right, but don't get any more, will you? The poor fish will be getting crowded in there."

After her father had gone Ai Lien went over to the fish-bowl. "That was a lie," she said. "I lied to Daddy. I've never done that before. How I wish you'd let me tell him about you!"

The fourth goldfish swam up to the surface and changed back into a dragon. "Oh, very well! Tell him!"

"Do you mean that?" asked Ai Lien, pleased.

"Yes, yes! Tell him at once."

Ai Lien ran out into the hall. "Daddy!" she called. "That new goldfish isn't really a goldfish, you know. It's the dragon in disguise!"

Mr. Feng looked up at her from the downstairs hall where he stood, talking with Grandmother. "Is it really?" he asked.

"His name's Lung Wang," Ai Lien told him, "and he's the son of the Dragon King of the Yangtze River."

"Fancy that now!" said her father. He said something to Grandmother and she laughed.

"I don't think they believed me," said Ai Lien to Lung Wang when she returned to her room.

"I knew they wouldn't," said the dragon. "The adult humans think you're just pretending."

"Well, at least I told him the truth," said Ai Lien. "Oh, Lung Wang, what fun this is going to be! I haven't had any friends for such a long time now, and I was getting awfully lonely. Now I've got a real *dragon!* That's even better!"

Lung Wang puffed himself up. He looked extremely pleased.

Chapter three

Dragon Magic

The following days were happy ones for Ai Lien. Although the situation at school did not improve, she no longer cared about it so much. It is hard to be unhappy when you have a talking dragon at home waiting for you — when you have a secret that nobody else knows, which would amaze everyone if only you were to tell it. Ai Lien hugged herself with delight all through school just thinking of it, and watched the clock eagerly as the slow hours wore on.

It was a hard secret to keep. For one thing, Ai Lien had difficulty explaining her sudden craving for seafood to her parents. Whenever her mother went shopping Ai Lien begged her to buy lots of fresh fish, shrimp and crabs. Then at dinner she would hide half her portion in her napkin when her parents were looking the other way, and would sneak it up to Lung Wang as soon as the meal was over. Mr. and Mrs. Feng were astonished at the speed with which the food vanished from her plate.

"Oh, well, she's a growing girl," said Mrs. Feng.

Sometimes Ai Lien went shopping with her grandmother after school. She would take along her pocket money, and when they went to the grocer's she would wait until Grandmother was busy examining the vegetables or trying to decide which spices to use in her cooking. Then Ai Lien would quickly buy something for Lung Wang — a can of salmon or tuna fish, or a battered tin of clams from the marked-down counter. The little dragon thrived and grew — literally right before her eyes. Ai Lien had never heard of anything growing quite so fast. By the middle of October he had more than doubled in size, and was about as big as a puppy.

"Dragons grow quickly because we are magical," he explained to her.

"How big will you get?" asked Ai Lien curiously.

"Very big indeed — larger than an elephant. Don't look so alarmed! By then I'll be back in the Yangtze River, in my father's palace." He waddled about the room on his stumpy little legs, which had only just grown out a week ago. "My parents, the Dragon King and Queen, will be very pleased to see what good care you've taken of me. They will probably reward you well."

But Ai Lien didn't want any reward. To her it was reward enough to look after Lung Wang, to watch him change and grow, and to be his friend. The two hours after school before her parents came home had always been rather lonely ones for Ai Lien. Now she had a friend to share the time with, and it seemed to go twice as fast. She and Lung Wang would spend the precious hours talking, telling stories, or looking at her father's books while Grandmother napped on the sofa.

Lung Wang would gaze with longing at the pictures of the Yangtze River in her father's books. He said they made him homesick, for even though he had still been inside his egg when he had been taken away from the Yangtze, his parents had told him all about it.

"Is the Yangtze the biggest river in China?" Ai Lien asked.

"No," admitted Lung Wang reluctantly. "The Huanghe, which you call the Yellow River, is the longest. But it isn't half as beautiful as my Yangtze, with its green gorges. Its waters teemed with dragons, centuries ago, as many of them as carp in a fishpond! But in the modern age, men started dropping explosives into the river, to blow up all the sharp rocks that made it difficult for ships to pass through. So of course the dragons left. Would *you* stay at home if somebody started dropping dynamite all over *your* neighbourhood? Why, the dragons had to put some very powerful spells on the royal palace, to prevent *it* from getting blown up, too!"

As well as the books about China, her parents had books on Canada and other countries, books about animals and nature, books of myths and legends from all over the world, including China. One day they came across a picture of the magic Hare of the Moon. "But there aren't any animals in the moon," said Ai Lien.

"There is just the one animal, as a matter of fact," replied Lung Wang. "Haven't you ever heard of the Hare of the Moon, who pounds the elixir of life with his pestle under the magic cassia tree? And Heng O, the moon goddess?"

Ai Lien laughed. "Those are only stories! There aren't any trees in the moon, or people. Men have gone up to the moon, you know — they went up years ago, before I was even born, in a great big rocket. Do you know what a rocket is?"

"Of course I do," replied Lung Wang. "It was your own people, the Chinese, who invented rockets and firecrackers, ages ago."

"But this was an enormous one, big enough to carry men inside," Ai Lien explained. "They blasted off into space, went to the moon and walked around on it, and didn't see anything at all there but rocks and dust."

"Were these rocket-men princes or sorcerers?"

"No — just ordinary men, like Daddy."

"Well, there you are then! You can't expect Madame Heng O and Gentleman Hare to introduce themselves to ordinary mortals! Only persons of some importance would have that honour."

Ai Lien had never thought of that. "I'm glad you're going to be here for a while," she told the dragon shyly. "You say such interesting things. If school were this much fun I wouldn't mind going! Look how much I've learned already."

One day Mrs. Jenkins told the class that they would each have to write a report on a subject of their choice, which they would then read aloud. Ai Lien told Lung Wang about it when she got home.

"I'm trying to decide what to do it on," she said.

"Why don't you do it on dragons?" suggested Lung Wang.

Ai Lien hesitated, remembering how the other children had laughed at her in science class. "I don't think they would believe what I told them," she replied. "And anyway you dragons want to be kept secret, don't you? I think I'll do it on China."

She and Lung Wang worked on the report for the next few days. The dragon was extremely helpful, especially with the parts on magic and legends.

"There! It's done," said Ai Lien on the evening before it was due. "How interesting it all is, too — I'm sure the teacher will like it. I can't wait for tomorrow."

"Who are you talking to, Ai Lien?" asked her father, outside the door.

"My dragon," Ai Lien replied as Lung Wang moved hastily toward the fish-bowl.

"Oh, that's all right then," said Mr. Feng.

Ai Lien gave her report at the end of the school day. She spoke of China's history first, starting with the Hsia dynasty around 2200 BC, and then listed all the other dynasties until the time of the last emperor. Then she moved on to geography, explaining that China was the third-largest country in all the world, after Russia and Canada. She spoke of tall pointed hills and icy mountains, long winding rivers and beautiful tropical gardens. She spoke of the people of China: "one-fifth of the world's population," she explained. She talked about all the customs, the Harvest Festival and the Dragon Boat Festival and the Chinese New Year. She talked about gods and goddesses: Heng O, the moon goddess and her husband, Yi, who lived in the sun, and Yu Huang-ti, the Jade Emperor of Heaven. And all this time the children sat very still and listened, their eyes wide.

"Very good, Ai Lien," approved Mrs. Jenkins when she had finished. "That was well-researched. You tend to mix up the imaginary things — myths and legends and so on — with the real-life things; they should really be kept apart. But it was very interesting and well presented. Well done."

Ai Lien hoped the other kids might be a little friendlier, since they had seemed so fascinated by her report. Some of the cleverer ones smiled at her as she took her seat again. But Mei whispered loudly to Patti that she knew a lot more about China than Ai Lien did, and she was going to do a project that would be "a thousand times better" than Ai Lien's. Jake Bradley was worse than ever. Mrs. Jenkins was called to the office, and as soon as she was out of the room he announced that Ai Lien had copied her report from a book, word for word, and that he was going to tell the teacher on her. Then after class he followed Ai Lien out into the hall, where she was getting a drink from the drinking-fountain.

"Hey, Alien," he shouted, coming up behind her, "it's five cents to drink from the fountain." He held his grubby hand out. "Pay up, or else."

Ai Lien stared at him. "What are you talking about? The fountain isn't yours."

When she turned around again he shoved her, hard, so that the water went not only into her mouth but also into her eyes and nose. She spun around with a cry of fury, wiping her face. "Stop it — *stop* it! Why won't you just leave me alone!"

"What's the matter here?" asked Mrs. Jenkins, coming out of the classroom.

"Aw, I just bumped into Ai Lien and she's making a big fuss," lied Jake.

"That's not true! He pushed me!" cried Ai Lien. She turned to Ben Davidson, who had been standing nearby. "You saw! Tell her what happened!"

Ben opened his mouth, but suddenly Jake was in front of him, looking at him through narrowed eyes. The smaller boy swallowed and said, "Uh — he bumped into her."

"See?" said Jake, spreading his hands out.

"All right then," said Mrs. Jenkins. She turned to Ai Lien. "No more shouting in the hall, if you please. There are still some classes going on."

The walk home was one of the worst Ai Lien had ever had. Jake followed her, jeering and laughing and calling her names.

"Hah — got you in trouble with the teacher!" he crowed in delight. "And that's only the beginning, Alien! You just wait — there's a lot worse to come!"

Even when Ai Lien got home and ran inside, slamming the door, Jake hung around on the sidewalk shouting insults. "Hey, Alien — Alien-From-Another-Planet!"

"Who is that loud and disruptive person?" asked Lung Wang when she brought him his bowl of tuna.

"It's Jake Bradley," she replied with a sigh. "He's the school bully and he hates me, I don't know why. I wish he could see you — that would frighten him away!"

"I've no intention of revealing myself to a lowly person like him," replied Lung Wang, tucking into the tuna.

"Hey, Alien!" yelled Jake from outside. "You're the ugliest girl in town!"

"Ignore him," advised Lung Wang, as tears came to Ai Lien's eyes.

"Hey!" Jake shouted. "Have you seen any dragons lately? Are they as ugly as you are?"

Lung Wang sat bolt upright at that. "Impudent

mortal!" he spluttered, spraying bits of tuna in all directions. "Insufferable barbarian!"

"Just ignore him," Ai Lien couldn't resist saying.

"I'll do nothing of the kind!" growled the dragon. He stared up at the sky outside the window. A strange glow shone from his green eyes, which had narrowed to slits.

All of a sudden a black cloud appeared out of nowhere, boiling across the sky and blotting out the sun. There was a rumble of thunder, low and menacing, and a wind blew down the street, tossing pieces of paper high into the air. Lightning flickered overhead.

Jake looked up in alarm. He started to run, but it was no use: before he was halfway down the street the rain came down in lashing torrents, soaking him to the skin.

"Lung Wang! *You* did that!" cried Ai Lien in amazement.

"Of course I did," Lung Wang replied. "I told you dragons had power over the weather. That was my very first rain-spell. I think it went rather well, don't you?"

They watched as the soaking wet Jake made off down the street, cursing. Suddenly they both began to laugh.

"Lung Wang," said Ai Lien, wiping tears from her eyes — tears of laughter now, rather than misery — "Lung Wang, you're *wonderful!*"

Lung Wang agreed.

They watched as the soaking wet Jake made off down the street, cursing.

That night after dinner Ai Lien sat down on the arm of her father's chair, where he had settled to read the newspaper. "Daddy, were you ever picked on when you were a kid?" she asked.

Mr. Feng lowered his paper. "Oh, are there bullies at your new school?"

"Yes," said Ai Lien. "At least, there's one. His name is Jake Bradley and he's really mean to everyone."

Mr. Feng looked thoughtful. "You have to feel sorry for bullies in a way. You see, Ai Lien, bullies are people who don't really like themselves. So they pick on people who are smaller than they are, to make themselves feel big and strong. It's pathetic, really. I remember there was a boy at my old school who used to call me names and try to get me to fight with him, but I just ignored him and when he saw he wasn't getting any reaction from me he gave up."

"Tell your teacher if he gets to be a problem," advised Mrs. Feng as she came into the room. "But as kids get older, bullying sort of falls off. They outgrow it."

"I think bullies must have been different when Daddy and Mummy were little," said Ai Lien to Lung Wang when she went up to her bedroom. "I can't see Jake going away just because someone ignored him." She sighed. "Mummy said she'd drive me to school if I wanted. But if Jake and the other kids see me coming to school in a car, they'll think I'm afraid of them. And I am," she admitted honestly. "But I won't let them know it."

"You are a person of great fortitude," said Lung Wang, impressed.

"What does 'fortitude' mean?" she asked.

"It means courage — bravery."

The look in the dragon's green eyes was admiring, and it gave Ai Lien a warm feeling.

Chapter four

The Sleeve Dog

Autumn wore on into winter. The red and golden leaves dropped from the trees, leaving the branches black and bare. Snow began to fall, lightly at first in flurries of big feathery flakes, then more heavily, covering up lawns and streets and sidewalks with its smooth whiteness. Winter coats and boots came out of closets, and the evenings seemed twice as long because it got dark earlier. How Ai Lien loved coming home after school, shutting the front door on the cold white world outside and running upstairs to her small cosy room. And now there was not only warmth and comfort to run up to, but Lung Wang as well.

The dragon had grown steadily through the passing

months, and was now the size of a full-grown dog rather than a puppy. His legs were longer and quite well developed, with hooked claws like a bird's. His gold and red scales gleamed as though they'd been polished. He was really very beautiful, as Ai Lien told him often.

But Lung Wang seemed very restless, now that winter had come. He walked from one end of the room to the other on his strong new legs, uttering deep sighs and throwing longing glances out the window.

"What's wrong, Lung Wang?" Ai Lien asked him one afternoon. She was at her desk doing homework, while he paced back and forth on the rug behind her.

He sighed. "I think I am just bored, that's all. It's hard for a dragon to be confined in this way. I spend most of my time in this little room, with only a few hours downstairs when your parents are out working. Dragons are used to being free, and I can only see the world from your window. It's hard to stay indoors when so many interesting things are outside."

Ai Lien leaned her chin on her hand, looking thoughtful. "Why don't you put on one of your magic disguises, then? Turn yourself into a human person, and walk around in the streets. That way you could go out all you like, and no one would know that you're really a dragon."

"I thought of that," said Lung Wang. "But I'm too nervous to try it. What if people talked to me — if someone asked me something that I ought to know, and became suspicious when I couldn't answer? I still don't know enough about this country of yours and its people to be able to pretend I'm one of them. And suppose the neighbours noticed a perfect stranger going in and out of your house, and talked to your parents about it? No, it's too risky."

Ai Lien had a bright idea then. "Well, why don't you change into an animal — a dog, for instance? Then I could take you out for walks after school and on weekends, and nobody would expect you to answer any questions!"

"A *dog*?" repeated Lung Wang in an ominous tone of voice. "Did I hear you correctly? I, Lung Wang, son of the Dragon King of the Yangtze River, turn myself into a *dog*?"

"Yes," replied Ai Lien eagerly. "I think it would be fun. I've always wanted a dog of my own."

Lung Wang drew himself up, his eyes blazing like green flames. A long roll of thunder boomed overhead, causing passers-by to stare up in astonishment at the clear winter sky. But then Lung Wang suddenly went still, the fire dying out of his eyes; he was gazing at the window, at the tree branches tossing about. A little brown bird fluttered by on some wind-blown errand of its own. From the street below came a variety of sounds: cars slushing past, people laughing and talking. Far away, a dog barked.

Ai Lien was staring at the window too, though she was more interested in the frost patterns on the panes — like a forest of crystal ferns, she thought dreamily, and wandered through it for a while in her imagination. Suddenly she heard a sound that brought her back from the frost-forest to her own room: a peculiar whining that didn't sound at all like Lung Wang. She turned to him, concerned — and then sprang up in amazement, for there in the middle of the floor stood the most beautiful little dog that she had ever seen.

His coat was a soft golden colour, like a sunset, and there was a thick downy ruff around his short little neck that made her think of a lion's mane. His eyes were like black shiny buttons, and his face was nearly flat, with a blunt muzzle and a broad grinning mouth. His tail was very soft and curly, and a lighter colour than the rest of him. Its creamy, plumelike tip curled right up over his back.

"Oh!" Ai Lien gasped. "Lung Wang, is that *you*? I've never seen a dog like that before! What kind is it?"

*. . . there in the middle of the floor stood the most
beautiful little dog . . .*

"The dog that I am now," came Lung Wang's voice out of the little dog's grinning mouth, "is known in this country as a Pekingese, although in China the breed has many different names. It is known as the lion dog, sun dog or sleeve dog."

"Why *sleeve* dog?" Ai Lien asked.

"Long ago, it was the custom for elegant ladies of the Imperial court to carry these small dogs about in their sleeves. I decided," Lung Wang added somewhat bitterly, "that if I must be a dog, I can at least be one of a respectable breed."

"I'd love to carry you around in *my* sleeve," exclaimed Ai Lien. "Would you mind very much if I petted you? Your fur looks so soft — "

"Oh, very well," assented Lung Wang with a sigh, and he let her gather him up in her arms and stroke his silky fur.

"I'll take you out right now," Ai Lien offered. "But I'll have to buy you a leash and collar first."

"*A leash and collar?*" echoed Lung Wang in horror.

"It's the law," Ai Lien explained apologetically. "It would be awful if a dogcatcher took you away!"

"A leash and collar," repeated the dragon dismally. "Well, why not, after all? I'm sure this is only the first of many such indignities I shall be subject to in this form."

Ai Lien told her grandmother that she was going out for a walk. She pulled on a coat and boots. Then holding the Pekingese very close to her she slipped him past Grandmother. Once outside they set off together through the snow.

"I guess I really shouldn't be out on my own like this," she told Lung Wang as they headed toward Dundas Street.

"You could hardly be safer than with a dragon," he retorted.

First she took Lung Wang to a pet store and fitted him out with a collar and leash, the nicest ones Ai Lien's savings could afford. Then they continued along the wintry streets. People smiled to see the little girl walking her dog. If they had looked more closely, however, they might well have wondered if she really were walking him, and not the other way around. Lung Wang was very impatient to see all there was to be seen, and he walked well in front of Ai Lien, straining at his lead to let her know in which direction he wanted to go. It was all she could do to keep up with him.

"How does it feel to be a dog?" she asked him curiously when there was no one around to hear.

"Most peculiar," he replied. "I keep having a nearly irresistible impulse to bark at things."

Ai Lien's neighbourhood was known as Chinatown, because there were so many Chinese people living there. All the stores and restaurants had signs that were written in Chinese as well as English, and there were wonderful open-air markets. Here there were food stalls right on the sidewalk, full of fascinating things: fruits and vegetables from faraway places, fresh fish, squid and crabs. The air smelled of the different kinds of food, as well as the incense smoke blowing from some of the shops. It was all very exciting.

Lung Wang enjoyed it immensely. He was intrigued by everything he saw, stopping often to stand on his hind legs and peer in windows, and getting Ai Lien to pick him up so that he could see into the ones that were too high for him. She had to wait for a long time in front of the windows of a jewellery store while he gazed in fascination at the rings and bracelets and necklaces, unwilling to leave.

"We dragons are strongly attracted to gemstones," he confessed as they finally walked away. "It's one of the few things we had in common with our barbarian Western cousins, the fire-breathing dragons — who are now extinct, fortunately."

One very grand store window had the most wonderful pieces of carved jade in it. Ai Lien had always loved passing by this store. There were trees of jade, with all their leaves and fruits and branches delicately carved, and long-tailed birds perching in them. There were lions that held loose, round balls in their mouths, lion and ball alike carved from the same piece of stone; and horses and cranes and dragons and carp. There were other interesting things as well: tiny landscapes with trees and houses all carved out of cork and set under glass globes, and vases and statues and figurines of china and of wood. Ai Lien and Lung Wang pressed their faces to the window and stared for all they were worth.

"What splendid jade!" Lung Wang approved. "Jade, you know, is really water, transformed into stone long ago by the gods."

"Is that *really* true?" she asked wistfully.

"Well, that's what my parents told me," he replied.

"It's a nice story anyway," said Ai Lien.

They walked on, westward along Dundas, stopping every now and then to gaze at some wonder or other. One store had embroidered robes similar to the one Ai Lien's father had brought her from China. One large black one had a red-and-gold dragon on it, not unlike Lung Wang.

"An Imperial dragon," he told her. "See, it has five claws on each foot. Most of us dragons have four claws, or three. The Imperial dragons were the Emperor's guardians: in the old days, if anyone but the Emperor wore a robe with a five-clawed dragon on it he could have been thrown into prison, or worse."

"That's very interesting," Ai Lien said, "but, oh, Lung Wang, please be careful! A talking dog is just as strange as a dragon, you know. If people overhear you they'll begin to wonder about you."

They walked on, past a large building with a fancy front and two huge lions carved of white stone set at either side of the door. People were going up and down the steps.

"What a majestic edifice!" cried Lung Wang. "It must be a great temple, to have such splendid decorations as that!" And he pulled so hard at the leash that Ai Lien lost her hold on it, and before she could stop him Lung Wang had run into the building, dodging around people's legs and through the open door.

"No! Lung Wang, wait!" shouted Ai Lien, and she ran after him.

She found herself in a grand hallway, with potted plants everywhere and red paper on the walls. At the end of the hall, great doors opened onto an enormous room, all red and gold, with tasselled lanterns hanging from the ceiling. At its far end was a platform with pillars at either side, and the pillars had great, golden dragons wound about them with bulging light bulbs for eyes. On the wall behind the platform was a golden screen with the figures of a dragon and a *feng-hwang* bird upon it. It really was a magnificent place.

Ai Lien saw the little dragon-dog padding across the red-and-gold carpet and pounced on him at once, lifting him in her arms. His small furry body was trembling with excitement.

"It is a dragon temple!" he whispered ecstatically in her ear. "Look at those glorious likenesses of my people wound around the pillars! And the golden screen! I had thought your people had forgotten all about us dragons nowadays. I see now that I was wrong. We are still revered, even in this faraway foreign land! But — " he added in puzzlement, "why are so many people *eating* in here?"

The room was filled with round tables, and whole families were seated around them, enjoying their spring rolls and shark fin soup and all kinds of rice dishes. Ai Lien hesitated; she had not had time to explain to Lung Wang that the sign over the door outside had read "Golden Dragon Restaurant." Now he was so happy and excited that she hated to disappoint him.

"Won't these people be overjoyed to find that they

have a real dragon in their midst?" he continued blissfully. "I will reveal myself to them immediately!"

"No, don't!" cried Ai Lien, as she imagined the pandemonium even a small dragon would cause among these unsuspecting diners. "You'll frighten them all terribly! This isn't a dragon temple, it's a — "

Just then a waiter came up to them. "Excuse me, little girl, but you cannot bring your dog in here," he told her politely but firmly.

"I — I'm sorry," she replied hastily. "I lost hold of the leash and he ran in — " And she whisked herself and Lung Wang out of the restaurant before he had a chance to protest.

It took her a long time to explain the situation to the dragon once they were safe outside, and even then he didn't seem to understand.

"Why don't they eat in their own homes?" he objected. "Are they all such bad cooks?"

Before she could come up with an answer to this, a loud voice shouted behind her: "Yahh! Alien!"

She jumped. It was Jake Bradley! Without turning to look she fled, clutching the Pekingese close to her chest as she ran.

"What is it?" asked Lung Wang, looking over her shoulder. "Oh, it's that despicable barbarian again."

"What does 'despicable' mean?" she asked, panting.

"It means thoroughly unpleasant."

Ai Lien had to agree that that was an excellent description of Jake.

"He appears to be gaining on us," the dragon added.

"Oh, no!" said Ai Lien, looking back. "He's too fast for me . . . Lung Wang, whatever you do, don't talk!"

Jake ran in front of her and Ai Lien had to stop.

"Ha, caught you!" he jeered.

"Leave me alone," said Ai Lien unhappily.

"Leave me alone!" imitated Jake in a high whining voice, and laughed. "You can't do anything, Alien. We're off school property."

Ai Lien made no answer.

Jake stared at Lung Wang. "What's that you've got there — a dog? You steal it from somewhere, hey?"

"Of course I didn't steal him," retorted Ai Lien indignantly.

"Liar," said Jake. He looked closely at Lung Wang, who was growling ominously. "Call that a dog? Looks more like an overgrown rat!"

That was enough for Lung Wang. In a flash he was out of Ai Lien's arms and had fastened his sharp little teeth in Jake's ankle.

"Hey — ow, ow! Help!" yelled Jake, leaping about and

trying to shake the Pekingese off. Lung Wang hung on, snarling.

Jake stumbled and fell in the snow, and Lung Wang jumped back with his fur bristling. Showing his teeth, he growled again as the boy rose. Jake backed away, snivelling. "Call him off — call him off!" he sobbed.

Ai Lien stared at the boy. He's a *crybaby*, she realized in amazement.

Jake got to his feet and ran off, limping. But Lung Wang was not about to let him off so lightly. He pursued the bully down the street, yapping furiously. To see big, fierce Jake running from the tiny creature was a wonderful sight. Ai Lien found that she was laughing uncontrollably.

"Come back, Lung Wang, come back," she called as soon as she had the breath. He returned to her, trailing the leash and looking pleased with himself.

"What a nice little dog!" exclaimed a lady in the street as Ai Lien and Lung Wang were heading home through the winter dusk. "I've never seen one quite like him."

"He *is* . . . unusual," Ai Lien agreed.

When her parents came home Ai Lien showed them the Pekingese dog and explained, with perfect truth, that she was looking after him for someone. "It'll be for quite a while, if that's all right," she said.

"Oh, are these people out of the country?" asked Mrs. Feng.

"Yes, in China," Ai Lien answered — after all, that's where the Dragon King and Queen *were*. Really, it was most convenient the way her parents kept supplying her with explanations.

Chapter five

The Dragon Dance

Winter wore slowly on. The snow in the street turned to slush, brown and gritty, and was covered by more snow. Icicles hung glittering from the eaves, puddles turned to patches of smooth, glassy ice. There were big storms with winds that howled around the house at night, making Ai Lien glad she had a safe, warm home to live in. She would snuggle down into her cosy bed, listening to the steady drone of the furnace. It was, she thought, as though the house were a big contented animal, purring to itself in its sleep. And it was nice to know that Lung Wang was there in the room with her, curled up by the heat register, sharing the warmth and cosiness.

Lung Wang by now had grown quite large — "as big as a pony," said Ai Lien in awe. As a result he was rather uncomfortable in Ai Lien's little bedroom, and spent more time than before in the shape of a Pekingese. Ai Lien's parents took her dog-sitting duties very seriously, to Lung Wang's annoyance: when they were home they saw to it that he was taken for walks in all kinds of weather and was given bowls of canned dog food which he had to eat in front of them. He was even bathed occasionally in a basin. Not that he minded the baths (dragons being water-dwelling creatures), or the walks or even the dog food so very much (now that he had a dog's sense of taste). But of course it was all very degrading for the son of a Dragon King to be treated as if he were a mere pet.

"Just think of it as a disguise," said Ai Lien. "It's kind of exciting really — as if you were a spy in a foreign country, or something like that."

"Exciting," replied Lung Wang as he gloomily surveyed a plate of dog biscuits, "is hardly the word *I* would have chosen."

As January drew to a close, there was an early thaw and much of the snow melted away. The days were longer now, the light lingering well into the evenings. The Chinese New Year was just around the corner.

Ai Lien loved the New Year holiday, which in the Chinese tradition came long after January first, near the end of the month, or in early February. Each year in the Chinese calendar was named for one of twelve symbolic animals: snake, horse, sheep, monkey, rooster, dog, pig, rat, ox, tiger, rabbit or dragon. The year that was now ending had been the Year of the Rabbit; this new, incoming year would be the Year of the Dragon. Beautiful banners and posters decorated with dragons were hung all over Chinatown in honour of the upcoming festival.

"A dragon year! Most auspicious!" approved Lung Wang when he saw them.

"What does 'auspicious' mean?" asked Ai Lien.

"It means very lucky, promising good fortune. Each year, you know, takes on the character of the animal it's named after. A Dragon Year is as different from other years as dragons are different from other animals."

All through the last month of the old year the Fengs, like every other Chinese family, made their New Year's preparations. The house was cleaned and dusted thoroughly, beautiful painted hangings were placed on the walls and red paper lanterns hung from the ceilings. Special foods for the holiday feast were bought and put away. In the kitchen was hung a sign with the name of the Kitchen God written on it in Chinese letters, and below it were placed candles and sticks of fragrant incense.

In the Chinese tradition, every home has its own company of little gods and spirits, to protect the house and the people in it. There is a god for every room of the house, even one to watch over the front door. The Kitchen God has a special part to play: he spends his days watching over the household, and when the old year is drawing to a close he rises up into heaven to make his yearly report to the Jade Emperor, Yu Huang-ti. Everything that anyone in the family did, good or bad, was made note of and taken into account at the heavenly court.

"I wouldn't worry, Ai Lien," Mr. Feng told her with a smile, "you've been a good girl all year."

Ai Lien smiled back happily, and when her father placed the traditional offerings of food below the Kitchen God's shrine she added some sweets that she had bought with her allowance. When she was a little girl, she had often tried to imagine what the Fengs' Kitchen God must look like. He would be an old man with a long beard, she had decided, and a rather stern expression, but there would be the hint of a twinkle in his eye too, as though he took his duties seriously but was really quite fond of the little household to which he had been assigned.

"Look, Mummy — we're giving the Kitchen God his sweets and things," Ai Lien told her mother, who had just come into the kitchen. "He's leaving for heaven very soon, to make his report."

Her mother laughed. "It sounds like bribery to me!"

"What's 'bribery'?" Ai Lien asked. Lung Wang, who was sitting nearby, opened his Pekingese mouth and then shut it again hurriedly.

"Bribery is giving people things so they'll do whatever you want," explained her father, grinning.

"Oh, no," replied Ai Lien earnestly. "That isn't it at all! You see, heaven is such a long way away — we must give him a good meal before his journey."

"Exactly," her father agreed.

Ai Lien watched the smoke rising from the sweet-smelling incense sticks. She almost imagined that she could see the Kitchen God, smiling his wise kindly smile, floating up in the air like the smoke, up through the roof above into Heaven.

"You see, Ai Lien," her father said, smiling as he saw the candlelight reflected in her big dark eyes, "this is magic, and magic needs people, just as people need magic. You can't have the one without the other. If people forget the magic, it'll vanish away forever, beyond recall. And people will be poorer without it."

She nodded, her eyes shining. Beside her Lung Wang too was staring thoughtfully at the shrine. "What a bright little fellow," remarked Mr. Feng. "You'd almost swear he knew what was going on."

This alarmed Lung Wang, who immediately began to be as doggy as he could, wagging his tail and licking Mr. Feng's hand and doing all sorts of things that would later embarrass him very much to recall.

The Kitchen God, it is said, returns to his household on New Year's Day, and then the festivities can begin. The Fengs celebrated in style, as always. There was a special holiday dinner, including a whole roast chicken and fish, several kinds of vegetables, noodles, nuts and little sweet cakes. Grandmother came over from next door to share the dinner with them, since the New Year celebration is a time for families to be together. Lung Wang had to be content with table scraps, but Ai Lien saved up some extra-nice ones for him. And as always, on this one night of the year, she was allowed to stay up past midnight.

The festivities and special observances didn't end with New Year's Day. Four days later there was "Argue

Day," when it was easier to have arguments than on any other day. It was better not to mingle too much with other people then. On the seventh day, all Chinese children were given presents of "lucky money" in bright red envelopes. But best of all, on the third day of the new year, there was the Dragon Dance.

Ai Lien was sure the Dragon Dance wouldn't be as much fun as it had in the past. After having known a real live dragon, she doubted that seeing a paper one would be at all exciting. All the same, when she and Lung Wang were hurrying toward Dundas Street that afternoon with her parents and grandmother strolling along behind, and she heard the beating of the drums and the clashing of the cymbals, and the loud bangs from the bursting firecrackers, and smelled the smoky smell on the air, she was surprised to feel the old excitement stirring inside her. She had the feeling that her heart had begun to beat in time to the drums, and that at any moment her feet would begin to dance all by themselves.

The dragon-dog's little black eyes were very bright, and his bushy Pekingese tail wagged constantly as they got closer and closer to the thrilling sounds. A string of bright scarlet firecrackers hanging from a tree branch nearby suddenly burst into a shower of smoke and sparks as they were passing by. People around them laughed and called out to one another.

"Kung hei fat choy!"

"Wishing you prosperity!"

The New Year's message was repeated on the big red banners hanging on the sides of all the buildings. The streets were thronging with people — not only Chinese but every imaginable kind of people, from all over the city. Everyone in Toronto, it seemed, had come to see the fun. There was even a man from a TV station filming everything.

Ai Lien looked eagerly around for the lion dancers: men wearing the brightly coloured paper heads of magical lions, whose fierce roars drive away evil spirits at the start of the new year. At the other end of the street she caught sight of some bright banners with dragons on them, swaying on poles above the heads of the crowd. The drums boomed. And then she saw a lion dancer — a bright flash of green, scarlet, blue and glittering gold as the paper head lifted high into the air and then dropped down out of sight.

Ai Lien and her family immediately hastened to the spot. The crowd was very thick here, with men, women and children all pressed close together at the side of the road, and Ai Lien had to pick Lung Wang up so that he could see. The brilliantly coloured head of the lion bobbed up and down as the two men inside the costume danced about. Lung Wang gave the special code-whine that meant he wanted to move forward, and Ai Lien slipped through the onlookers until they were closer to the front and could see more clearly.

The paper lion was playing a sort of game with another dancer. This man had a long piece of red cloth in his hands, and he would wave it in the air and then throw it so it fluttered to the ground. The lion would then pounce on the cloth, grip it in his cardboard jaws and toss his head about, whirling the cloth like a propeller, before flinging it back to the man. And all this time the drums and cymbals boomed and clashed, until the sounds got into Ai Lien's blood and she longed to dance, too.

Lung Wang was very excited by all this. He kept wriggling in Ai Lien's arms, as though he wanted to break free and join in the dance. It was all she could do to hold onto him.

Suddenly the lion turned away from the dance and headed off across the street, toward the shops that lined the sidewalk. His red, blue, green and gold cloth body rippled majestically as he mounted up the steps leading to a grocery store and began to dance again, pumping his head up and down and swaying from side to side in rhythm with the drum beats. This, Ai Lien knew, was the magic dance that drives all the bad spirits out of a place.

Then Ai Lien's parents and grandmother walked on, and she and Lung Wang had to follow them. They hadn't gone far before they met another crowd coming along the sidewalk toward them. And here at last was the dragon, a long coiling one made all of paper, with red glass eyes and golden horns, his long body supported on two poles carried by a pair of men. They were running after a third man, who carried upon another pole a great, round ball, painted gold and red. The dragon seemed to be chasing the painted ball: the men could make him move by raising and lowering the poles, so that he dipped and rolled and plunged in the air above their heads. Around and around the three men went, while the crowd laughed and cheered; and around and around with them went the dragon and the ball.

Lung Wang whined shrilly. "*I* should be doing that!"

"What did you say, dear?" asked Grandmother in Mandarin, turning to Ai Lien with one hand cupped around her ear. "I didn't quite hear."

"Oh, nothing, Grandmother," she replied, putting her hand hastily over the Pekingese's muzzle.

Her parents and grandmother walked away from the dragon dance and she followed, taking the reluctant Lung Wang with her. He really was in a strange mood, she thought with concern. Then all of a sudden he made a peculiar sound — a sort of whining bark — and leaped right out of Ai Lien's arms. In a moment he had vanished from sight in the crowd.

"Lung Wang! Lung Wang! Where are you?" Ai Lien cried, and turned to her parents. "Mummy, Daddy, the dra— I mean the *dog* ran away!"

The winter dusk had fallen and it was now quite dark. Ai Lien could not see Lung Wang anywhere. She and her parents went to and fro in the crowd, calling his name, but no little Pekingese dog came running up to them.

"Please," she said to a lady nearby, "have you seen my little dog, Lung? I can't find him anywhere."

Before the lady could reply there came a great shout from the crowd. People were yelling and waving their arms, pointing at something she could not see. The paper dragon, which had been dancing about on its poles, suddenly tipped over and collapsed to one side. For a moment all was noise and confusion. She could see the red and gold ball on its pole still moving above the crowd, but it was jogging along now at the most terrific speed, as if the man carrying the pole were running for all he was worth.

Just then she managed to squeeze past the people in front of her, and gave a loud gasp of dismay at what she saw.

The man with the ball was indeed running down the street at top speed. Behind him in hot pursuit came Lung Wang — not as a tiny Pekingese, but in his own dragon shape, red-and-gold scales gleaming. He was not chasing the man; his large, green, rather bulging eyes were fixed in fascination on the painted ball atop the pole.

The man, coming up against a mob of people approaching from the other end of the street, found he could flee no farther. He turned to gape with amazement at his pursuer. Shouts went up from the spectators.

Ai Lien called out despairingly, "Oh, no, Lung Wang! No!" But her cry was drowned in the uproar. She groaned. Lung Wang had given himself away! Now what was going to happen?

Just then she heard the man next to her say: "What an incredible costume!"

The others around him agreed.

"I've never seen anything like it, have you?"

"It's much better than the lion dancers' one. Looks almost real."

"I wonder who's inside it?"

Behind him in hot pursuit came Lung Wang — not as a tiny Pekingese, but in his own dragon shape . . .

Ai Lien learned something then; namely, that people who refuse to believe in something will often go right on disbelieving even if it appears right in front of their noses. The children around her were all watching with rapt, shining faces; but the grown-ups did not believe in dragons, and so they were absolutely determined that Lung Wang should be someone in a costume.

"Grown-ups are funny," she said to herself. "Lucky for Lung Wang!"

The dragon was prancing about now — doing the dragon dance, she realized. People shouted and pointed and laughed, but he didn't seem at all aware of them: his eyes were on the painted ball. The man, grinning now, began to dance with it, leading Lung Wang around and around with it as he had the fake dragon. Lung Wang followed, his eyes and mouth wide open.

And then Ai Lien heard someone say: "Where's that TV cameraman? He should be getting all this down on tape!"

Ai Lien gasped. Lung Wang on the TV news! It was exactly the sort of thing he'd said he wanted to avoid. His secret would be out if that were to happen, for someone would surely recognize him for what he was — a genuine, flesh-and-blood dragon! Really alarmed now, she ran forward and shouted urgently into Lung

Wang's ear: "Lung Wang! You must get out of here! They'll put you on TV, the magic mirror — everyone will know about you!"

He paid no attention to her, his eyes still fastened on the swaying ball. Desperate, she got in front of him, blocking his view, and repeated her warning.

The dragon halted. His glassy eyes suddenly focused themselves, his foolish grin vanished as his jaw dropped. He looked around wildly at the faces surrounding him, the pointing fingers and waving arms. Then with a loud yelp he turned and fled, darting between two parked cars to disappear into an alley, with several laughing spectators in hot pursuit.

"Where's he gone? Where did he go? He was absolutely marvellous!" people shouted. "Where's the man in the wonderful costume?"

"You talked to him," said a man to Ai Lien. "You know him, then?"

"Uh . . . yes, I know him," she replied.

"Who is he?"

"I can't tell you," she answered frantically. "It's a secret!"

Just then she saw, to her relief, the small familiar shape of a Pekingese dog come trotting out of the alley, all but unnoticed by the people who were still looking for the mysterious dragon-dancer. He crept up to Ai Lien and made no protests as she picked him up and hurried over to her parents and grandmother. Fortunately they had not seen Lung Wang's dragon dance, nor Ai Lien's odd part in it: they had been too far back in the crowd. Luck had certainly been on her side tonight.

"Gosh, that was close!" she whispered in the Pekingese's ear as she set him down on the ground again. Lung Wang said nothing. He was abashed at his loss of self-control and as Ai Lien and her family headed for home he slunk along at the end of his leash, carrying his curly tail as low as a Pekingese possibly can.

"I — ah — regret that loss of composure today," he said to her later when they had gone up to Ai Lien's bedroom and were safely out of hearing. "I was overcome at the sight of the pearl."

"What pearl?" Ai Lien asked drowsily. She would wish later that she had paid more attention to what he said, but it had been a long day and she was very tired.

"Why, the magic pearl — the big globe on the pole, you know," he answered. "Didn't you see it?"

He waited for Ai Lien to ask for more details, but then he saw that she had fallen asleep. Jumping up on the bed, he curled up on the coverlet and settled down to sleep, too.

Chapter six

Magical Misadventures

Winter was almost over now. The snow lay in patches on the ground, irregularly shaped like islands on a map, with the grass like a greenish brown sea in between. As the days went by the sea became greener, and the islands smaller and smaller. Then the crocuses decided that it was spring and unfurled their delicate petals: Ai Lien spied a whole clump of them, yellow and white and pale purple, growing in a sheltered place at the side of the house. The next day she looked out the window and saw a red-breasted robin hopping across the lawn, back from his winter vacation in the South, and she knew that it really was spring at last.

Lung Wang had grown a great deal in the past month

or so, and was now about the size of a horse, though much longer and narrower in shape. He couldn't possibly stay in Ai Lien's room these days unless he took the shape of a smaller animal. If he wanted to take his own shape, he had to wait until Mr. and Mrs. Feng left the house, and then go downstairs to the family room and turn back into a dragon there. Even then he had to curl himself up like a snake to fit into the space. If he stretched himself out, his head, neck and forelegs fit into the family room, while his long narrow body, hindlegs and tail spilled over into the dining room and the tip of his tail just reached into the kitchen. There he would stay until three-thirty in the afternoon, when Grandmother Feng came over to look after Ai Lien, and he had to hide again.

It was all very tiresome for him. Dragons are made for big open spaces, for the blue reaches of the sky and the depths of oceans and rivers; being cooped up in a small house designed for human beings made Lung Wang very uncomfortable. And so he spent most of his time transformed. As a goldfish he was able to associate with the other goldfish during the day when Ai Lien was at school. Since goldfish are descended from carp, and carp are related to dragons and can even, under special circumstances, become dragons, he did not mind this so very much. Indeed he told Ai Lien that he was instructing Jade, Pearl and Plum Blossom on the process of dragonification; he wasn't sure it would work on goldfish, but they were reportedly anxious to try it.

Grandmother Feng usually napped on the sofa in the afternoons, leaving Ai Lien and Lung Wang a precious hour or two in which the dragon could do as he pleased. But when Ai Lien's parents came home he had to take the shape of a Pekingese again. "It's a good thing my royal father and mother, the King and Queen of the Yangtze River, can't see me now!" he moaned to Ai Lien one day after school. "Going about with a collar and leash, eating dog food! What a comedown it is for me!"

Ai Lien liked Lung Wang's dog shape, but she did see his point. "It won't be much longer," she said, "now that the good weather is coming, you can live out of doors, and perhaps you can even take your own shape at night, when there's no one around to see."

"I've even begun to *think* like a dog," Lung Wang continued despairingly. "A cat walked across the lawn yesterday, and before I knew what I was doing I caught myself *barking* at it! Imagine!"

"Cheer up," said Ai Lien. "It's spring!"

"That's the worst of it," he replied. "My dragon blood is restless now. When winter comes to the lands of the

East, the dragons withdraw into the depths of the rivers. They stay at the river bottom all through winter."

"Like turtles," said Ai Lien with interest.

"Not at all like turtles," Lung Wang corrected a trifle huffily. "*Turtles* bury themselves in mud, whereas dragons go to their spacious and elegant palaces. And then, when the winter comes to an end, with the cracking of the ice, and the warming of the waters, and the long rays of the sun reaching down into the green depths — up they rise to the surface, and burst out in showers of white spray to soar up, up into the sky. And all the fresh spring air is full of the trumpeting cries of the dragons!"

Lung Wang stretched out to his full length, drew a deep breath, and gave a bellowing cry that rattled the windowpanes.

"Ow!" exclaimed Ai Lien, putting her hands to her ears. The cry rang in the air like a gong, even after Lung Wang had closed his jaws again. Grandmother stirred and muttered on the sofa.

"If you think *that* was loud," said Lung Wang, "imagine dozens of full-grown dragons, bigger than elephants, all roaring at once! Of course," he added, "they'd have to be careful nowadays, with so many humans about." He sighed deeply. "The thought of it makes me homesick."

"Well, I'm sure you'll be home again before long," Ai Lien told him, and now it was her turn to sigh. Lung Wang had only been with her for a few months now, and already she felt as if she'd always known him. His *chi'h muh* had not yet appeared on his forehead, but when it did she knew he would fly back home as fast as he could. She couldn't bear to think of what life would be like without her dragon friend.

Lung Wang's teeth had begun to fall out — "My baby teeth," he explained, seeing Ai Lien examining an ivory tusk one day. It seemed rather large for a "baby" tooth.

"It's a shame your people don't believe in dragons nowadays," he added. "I seem to recall my father saying something about dragons' teeth having marvelous healing powers. Ground up and made into medicine, they can cure everything from headaches to insanity."

"Really?" cried Ai Lien in amazement. "That's wonderful! You know, my mother has the most awful headaches sometimes. If only I could give her some dragon's tooth, it'd make her better."

"She wouldn't take it," said Lung Wang. "She'd think you were crazy."

"That's true," admitted Ai Lien. "I wish you'd show yourself to her."

"Then she'd think *she* was crazy," the dragon pointed out.

"Oh, well. Maybe I can slip some powdered dragon tooth into her food or something, next time she has a headache," Ai Lien suggested.

It so happened that the following week Mrs. Feng had one of her worst headaches and had to retire to bed, leaving Ai Lien and her father to have supper by themselves. After they had eaten and she had helped wash up Ai Lien went to her mother's room and knocked on the door softly.

"Mummy?" she said. "Is there anything you'd like? There's some food left for you, if you want it."

"No thank you, dear," replied her mother. "I just want to lie down for a while. I'm really not hungry."

"Couldn't I get you an Aspirin or something?" Ai Lien suggested.

"Thank you, I've already got some pills in here with me. But," Mrs. Feng added, "you could get me a glass of water to take them with, there's a good girl."

Ai Lien ran to the kitchen and filled up a glass, then tiptoed back to her own room. Lung Wang was there, curled up on the bed in his dog shape.

"What are you up to?" he inquired sleepily.

"I'm going to give Mummy some of your tooth," Ai Lien

replied. "She's got a headache."

"So! This is the great experiment," said Lung Wang, sitting up.

It took a long time to grind the tooth up — it was harder than she'd realized. But at last there were some tiny white bits of it floating in the glass.

"It's no good, it all sinks to the bottom," Ai Lien observed.

"Shake it up a little," the dragon suggested, interested now.

Ai Lien did, sloshing a bit of it in the process. The little white flecks floated briefly before settling to the bottom again.

"Oh, well, I'll have to give it a good shake before I give it to her, that's all," she said.

She took the glass to her mother. "Sorry it took so long," she apologized.

"Thank you, dear," said her mother, holding her hand out.

Ai Lien turned to one side quickly, and, putting her hand over the glass, gave it a quick shake. Her mother saw and stared. "What did you do that for?" she asked.

"Oh, I thought it might need it," replied Ai Lien vaguely.

Mrs. Feng took her pill and washed it down with some

water. "That's funny," she said, "the water's all gritty. Did you get it from the kitchen tap?"

"Yes," answered Ai Lien.

"It can't have been a very clean glass. Oh, well, never mind." Mrs. Feng lay down again and put the ice pack back on her head as Ai Lien slipped out.

The dragon's tooth must have been extremely powerful, for Mrs. Feng was completely recovered within the hour.

"The doctor was right," she said, pleased. "Those pills *did* work!"

Ai Lien was so impressed by the performance of the dragon's-tooth powder that she decided she must let the whole world know all about it. It wouldn't be fair to keep such a marvellous cure secret, she thought.

"Anyway," she told herself, "I don't have to tell people where the cure *came* from."

Ai Lien knew that there were a lot of hospitals along University Avenue, a big street not far from Chinatown. If she could cure a lot of sick people, she thought, the grown-ups would have to believe in the cure.

Ai Lien didn't quite like leaving her neighbourhood without a grown-up, but Lung Wang went with her, and as he had said before, you just couldn't be safer than with a dragon — even one disguised as a Pekingese.

Together they wandered up and down University Avenue looking at the hospitals. Ai Lien decided on one that was especially for sick children — children, she knew, would be more likely to believe in magical medicine than grown-ups. Unfortunately she had to leave Lung Wang outside, as dogs were not allowed in the hospital, but she got in behind a large group of people who were on their way to visit someone and tagged along with them down a long hallway with doors opening into rooms on each side. Ai Lien had quite a pleasant time going into room after room giving her magic powder to the children before a nurse came and caught her.

"Now then, out you go," said the nurse firmly.

"But it's a miracle cure," said Ai Lien desperately. "It cures everything from headaches to insanity!"

"That's right, dear!" replied the nurse in a bright, cheery tone. "Now why don't you go and play your nice game outside?"

It was no use, thought Ai Lien despairingly when she rejoined Lung Wang on the hospital steps. The grown-ups just didn't understand.

But she wouldn't give up. The next day she went to the corner store and bought a big piece of cardboard and a felt marker. She wrote on the cardboard:

MIRAKEL CURE FOR FREE!!
STOP HERE & GET SOME

Then she put out a table on the sidewalk with her sign in front, like the children who sold lemonade in summertime. But the people who went by only laughed at her sign — though that might have been at the way she spelled "miracle." Ai Lien wasn't sure she'd got it right.

"This is awful, Lung Wang," she finally said to the dragon when it became apparent that no one was going to take any of the powder. "No one will take any of the cure, even for free. Mummy hasn't had a headache for ages, but she thinks it's the doctor's pills that made her better. To think I've got a magical miracle cure and nobody will believe me!"

"That's humanity for you," sniffed Lung Wang. "You can never get people to take what's good for them."

That night Ai Lien's parents had a discussion after she was in bed.

"I'm really rather concerned about Ai Lien," said Mrs. Feng. "She doesn't seem to know where to draw the line between what's real and what's make-believe."

"I wouldn't worry," replied Mr. Feng. He had heard all about the miracle cure stand from the neighbours and thought it a tremendous joke.

"And there's this business about the dragon," went on Mrs. Feng.

"I think it's a delightful game," said Mr. Feng. "I told her about Chinese dragons and it's fired her imagination, that's all. My mother's *very* pleased about it: you know she's always felt, like me, that Ai Lien doesn't appreciate her own Chinese roots. Besides, didn't *you* have a pretend friend when you were small?"

"But Ai Lien is nine now," replied Mrs. Feng. "Don't you think she's getting a little old for that kind of thing?"

"Oh, I don't know," her husband answered. "Kids seem to be in such a hurry to grow up these days. Why can't they just enjoy being kids? They've got all the rest of their lives to be grown up. Let Ai Lien have her fun."

"But I wish she had some *real* friends," sighed Mrs. Feng. "She never brings anybody home from school to play. It doesn't seem right, that's all."

A few days later came the affair of the pearl. Of all the things that happened this was the strangest, the most alarming, and the one that came nearest to getting Ai Lien into serious trouble.

It all began very innocently, as such things often do. Grandmother had had to go to the dentist, so for once they had the house completely to themselves and Lung

80

Wang could take his own shape. Ai Lien was upstairs, feeling about underneath the dresser for a pencil she had dropped when her fingers encountered something unexpected, something smooth and round like a marble, only bigger. Surprised, she pulled the something out and had a close look at it, but she still couldn't say what it was; she'd never seen anything like it.

It was a little round globe about the size of a table tennis ball, all dusty from being under the dresser. Curious, she took it down to show to Lung Wang, but he was fast asleep, basking with his head and forepaws in a patch of sun, and looking so content that she didn't want to disturb him. Ai Lien took the mysterious object into the kitchen and washed it in the sink. Once the dust was all cleaned away it turned out to be very beautiful, white with touches of pink and blue in it, like a great pearl. When she held it under the water and it caught the sunlight it shimmered like a soap bubble, with all the colours of the rainbow. She left it in the sink and went back to Lung Wang, but finding him still napping she tiptoed quietly past him and went back upstairs. Grandmother had said she would be away for about an hour and a half, so Ai Lien decided she'd let the dragon sleep a little longer, then come down and wake him, and show him the beautiful globe.

She had had a long, exhausting day at school, with a double period of gym and a ball game afterwards, and she was very tired. Before long Ai Lien found herself nodding over her book. She knew she mustn't doze off, for Lung Wang would have to be awakened before Grandmother came home, or she'd find him there in his dragon shape. But Ai Lien was so comfortable in her cushioned chair, and the spring sunlight was so soothing, that she presently fell fast asleep.

While she slept Ai Lien dreamed that she was at a beach, wading in the ocean. The water was very cold, and her feet were beginning to feel quite chilled when she woke up. To her amazement she saw that she was up to her ankles in *water*. Her bedroom was flooded!

Ai Lien sprang up and splashed out into the hall. Water lay ankle-deep everywhere. When she got to the stairwell she saw that it was all filled up, with the steps and the downstairs hall looking all dim and wavery, as things do at the bottom of a pool.

"Oh no!" she gasped aloud. Whatever could have happened? Had a pipe burst somewhere? But even if one had, surely it shouldn't have filled up the whole house like this, so quickly!

What could she do? Ai Lien's mind started racing. If she knew how to swim, she might dive down to the front door to open it and let all the water out. But the door looked so far away — even if she had been a *good* swimmer, Ai Lien doubted she could hold her breath for that long. *It's a good thing Lung Wang is a dragon and can live underwater,* she thought suddenly. Where *was* Lung Wang, anyway?

The water was rising fast; in a moment it was over her knees. Ai Lien waded over to the little door that led to the attic and tried the handle: it wasn't locked. She dragged it open, and the water pushed it shut behind her as she raced up the stairs. But still the water rose; it got in under the door and followed her up the steps, swishing and gurgling.

"How awful!" she moaned. "What am I going to tell Mummy and Daddy?" She ran to the little attic window and tried to open it, thinking that this way at least the water would all run out the window, and not go right up to the ceiling. And maybe she could give the neighbours a shout. She smiled as another odd thought came to her: she had heard of people being rescued from *burning* houses, but not from *flooding* ones! Would the neighbours call the fire department? And what would the firemen do? A *hose* wouldn't be any help, that was certain!

The attic window was very rarely used, and was stiff

She had never been so glad to see him as at that moment.

and warped as a result. Ai Lien couldn't get it open, no matter how hard she tried. Suddenly the situation no longer seemed the least bit funny, and her eyes filled with tears. The water was nearly up to her waist now, and showed no sign of stopping.

"Lung Wang!" she cried out. "Oh, Lung Wang, where are you?"

There was a plopping sound beside her, and then another plop. Looking down into the water, Ai Lien saw her goldfish swimming about in it. Of course — they must have got out of their bowl when her room filled up. Her tears spilled over. Her precious room, with all her books and toys, all flooded!

And then, with a bubbling sound and a splash, Lung Wang's horned head and scaly coils rose up out of the water.

"Lung Wang!" Ai Lien waded over to the dragon and hugged him. She had never been so glad to see him as at that moment.

"What an extraordinary thing!" remarked Lung Wang. "I was asleep in the family room downstairs when I awoke to find myself underwater! The Apprentice Dragons and I have been having a splendid swim all over the house. They are enjoying it immensely — they're used to being cooped up in a fish-bowl, never getting to see the other rooms. I did wonder where *you'd* gone, though."

"Oh, Lung Wang!" sobbed Ai Lien. "What are we going to do? We're trapped!"

"Nonsense," replied Lung Wang. "I told you dragons have power over water. I can easily send it all away — if you're sure you don't want it? I find it quite a refreshing change, myself."

"Please, please make it go away!" begged Ai Lien. "Grandmother will be back any minute!" She could imagine her poor grandmother opening the front door — and being swept away down the street by an enormous wave!

"Oh, very well," said Lung Wang. He puffed himself up, his green eyes narrowed with concentration, then turned to the goldfish. "You'd best get back to your bowl, you three, or you'll find yourselves high and dry!" The Apprentice Dragons obediently swam away down the stairs. Already the water level was sinking. As she watched, it began to swirl down the staircase like bathwater going down a drain. In a moment the stairs were perfectly dry.

Ai Lien ran down them and into her room. The goldfish were back in their bowl and everything was back to normal. "It's all dry!" she cried in astonishment, touching the bedspread, the books, her stuffed animals. "I thought everything would be ruined."

"I told *all* the water to go away — every drop," Lung Wang explained. "The whole house should be back to normal now."

Ai Lien hugged him again in her delight. "Thank you, thank you! I don't know what I'd have done without you, Lung Wang! But," she added in puzzlement, "I can't understand how it happened in the first place."

"Neither can I," the dragon admitted, "but there's magic here, I can feel it."

The mystery was solved when they went downstairs to make sure that everything was in order, and Lung Wang found the little white ball still in the sink. She told him how she'd found it under the dresser, and had taken it downstairs to clean it.

"Was there water in the sink when you left it?" he asked.

"Yes," she said. "Why?"

"That explains it then," said Lung Wang. "This is my magic pearl."

"Your what?" she asked.

"Each dragon," Lung Wang told her, "has a special pearl, like an oyster's except the dragon's is made out of magic. Haven't you noticed that the dragons on vases and robes and things are almost always shown with a round object?"

"Yes, I always wondered what that was."

"It's meant to be the magic pearl. So was that red ball the dancer was carrying at New Year's. That's why I ran after him, you see — no dragon can resist a magic pearl, even an imitation one. I've had my own pearl since I was a baby, and it's grown since then, adding on new layers of magic and growing more and more powerful. I've been keeping it in a secret place, as dragons do. I really should have told you about it sooner."

"You tried to, once," said Ai Lien regretfully, remembering. "I should have listened. But why did the pearl cause a flood?"

"One of the magical properties of these pearls," Lung Wang explained, "is that they multiply things. If you were to place one in a bowl of rice, for example, you'd soon have heaps and heaps of rice. If you put one in a coin box, the box would overflow with more money than you could spend in your whole life. So when you put it in the sink, you see, it multiplied the water."

"That's amazing," said Ai Lien. But thinking of it somehow gave her a cold feeling. She wondered what would happen to her dragon friend if people found out about this power of his. They might even try to make a slave of him, she thought fearfully, and she told Lung Wang so.

"Of course," he replied. "That, my sagacious friend, is one of the reasons we dragons have drawn apart from humans. That, and your lamentable habit of dropping dynamite on our houses."

"I guess we humans make a mess of things," she said sadly.

"You *are* a peculiar race," Lung Wang agreed. Then he walked over and rested his tufted chin on her shoulder.

"Present company excepted, of course," he said kindly.

Chapter seven

Lung Wang Goes to School

Spring was slowly turning into summer. Ai Lien couldn't wait for school to end — although, with Lung Wang's help it hadn't seemed as bad as at the beginning of term, when her unhappiness had made her grades drop. She had found that she couldn't answer a lot of the questions he asked her about Canada and Western ways in general, so she had repeated the questions to her teacher and, in the process, learned a great deal herself.

"Your school work is improving," Mrs. Jenkins told her one day. "You weren't doing all that well for a while. Is someone helping you at home?"

"Yes," said Ai Lien. It was true. With Lung Wang's help she had begun to be interested in things again, and her marks were as high as they had been before she came to Thornwood. But summer vacation was calling to her now, as the days grew ever longer and warmer. In summer she'd be home all day while her parents worked, with only Grandmother to look after her. She and Lung Wang would have hours and hours together, instead of just the time between school and suppertime.

"Think of all the fun we'll have!" she told Lung Wang one day while they were sitting in the family room downstairs. At least, Ai Lien and about one-quarter of Lung Wang were in the family room; the rest of the dragon was sprawled through the dining room and kitchen. Grandmother had gone next door for a few minutes, so for the time being he was free to take his own shape.

"I have been thinking," Lung Wang announced suddenly, "that I would like to go to school."

"To *school!*" exclaimed Ai Lien. "What on earth for?"

"To learn," the dragon replied, tapping one claw thoughtfully on the floor. "I can't read very well yet, but from what you say school is mainly sitting and listening to what the teacher says. It would be a good way for me to find out more about the human world."

"They wouldn't let me bring a dog in though," Ai Lien

said. "You'd have to turn into a child to go to school."

"No, that wouldn't work," said Lung Wang. "Too many explanations needed. I'll have to think of something else."

The following day was something of a setback for Ai Lien. Standing up to Jake Bradley and ignoring his threats had become a habit with her, and in the past few weeks she had noticed that other kids were doing it, too. She was able to relax a little, and sometimes forgot about Jake altogether.

But he had not forgotten about her. That morning Ai Lien found her desk empty: all her textbooks had disappeared. She knew that Jake hadn't taken them himself — he was too much of a coward to risk being caught — but it was clear from his glee when Mrs. Jenkins scolded Ai Lien for her carelessness that Jake was behind the trick. At recess he came up to her, grinning.

"I know where your books are," he gloated, "and you can have them back for five dollars."

Ai Lien refused.

"Well, goodbye to all your books then," he jeered as he swaggered off.

"My father says people like you really hate themselves," she shouted after him. "You only act this way so you can feel strong. It's *pathetic*," she added.

He turned, scowling at her. "You just watch yourself," he snarled, "that's all. The fun's only beginning, Alien."

When Ai Lien got home from school she found the house locked up. She used her key to get in, and found a note from Grandmother on the kitchen table saying that she had to go out to the store for something. Lung Wang was nowhere in sight, which was unusual; in his dragon shape he was rather hard to miss. Perhaps he had changed into something else, Ai Lien thought. Lung Wang was becoming extremely good at shape-changing, with the aid of a book called *Animals of the World*, and he loved surprising her. She never knew these days what she would see when she went into her bedroom: an ostrich, a white rat, a crocodile, or a Jersey cow. Once, when Ai Lien had come home in tears after a particularly nasty day at school, he had turned himself into a pony and let her ride on his back. They hadn't dared go outdoors, so they'd had to be content with riding around the house: through the family room into the dining room, the dining room into the kitchen, the kitchen into the family room, all the time hoping the noise of hooves wouldn't wake up Grandmother. It really was a good thing for them that she liked her afternoon nap and was more than a little deaf!

93

Now Ai Lien walked slowly from one room to another, giggling nervously. "Lung Wang?" she called. "Where are you?" There was no answer. Ai Lien ran up to her room, but there was nothing there, and the three goldfish were alone in their bowl. She ran back downstairs again. "Lung Wang!"

A tiny sound, like the chirping of a cricket, came from somewhere down by her feet. Ai Lien glanced down and gave a gasp.

"Lung Wang! Is that *you*?" she exclaimed.

She stared in disbelief as the dragon scuttled toward her. Lung Wang had *shrunk*: he was smaller now than he had been when he was a baby!

"Lung Wang, what's happened to you?" she asked. "Is it magic again?"

"It is," he chirped, and puffing himself up, he slowly expanded right before her eyes to his normal size. "It's my shrinking-spell," he explained. "I only just discovered how to do it today. I've always known that dragons were supposed to be able to change their size — to be 'as small as a silkworm or as big as a cloud,' as my father put it. Now that I know how to do it I don't have to turn into an animal to fit into your house. And I can go to school."

"Of course!" said Ai Lien, excited. "You would fit in my

pocket! No one would know you were there, and you could hear everything! And — well, Jake's really bugging me, and some of the other boys too. But if I had *you* with me . . . " Her face brightened at the thought. Suddenly going to school tomorrow didn't seem half so bad.

It's possible to face almost anything, Ai Lien decided as she arrived at school the next morning, if only you have some company. She had abandoned her jeans and chosen a loose cotton dress to wear that day as it had big deep pockets, and Lung Wang assured her he was perfectly comfortable in the right-hand one.

Jake scowled as Ai Lien came skipping into the classroom. She was perfectly happy and not at all afraid, and didn't notice how Jake glared at her all morning, muttering under his breath. What did she care? She had a dragon in her pocket, who was a prince and magical besides! There was only one alarming moment, when Mrs. Jenkins asked the class a question and Lung Wang, forgetting himself, called out the answer in a tiny piping voice.

"What's that, Ai Lien?" Mrs. Jenkins asked. "Speak up a little, will you?"

At recess Ai Lien went off by herself as usual, to the little pine wood at the edge of the soccer field. She had always been a little sad when she wandered by herself among the trees. But today was different; today she had Lung Wang.

"Well," she said to him, as soon as she was sure that there was no one else around, "what do you think of school so far?"

The dragon poked his miniaturized head out of her pocket. "I find it highly instructive. I have learned a great deal about humans today, and about this curious northern country of yours. Geography and history were most informative."

"English class is fun," said Ai Lien. "I like reading all those stories. I don't like science as much, but I want to be a veterinarian when I grow up, so I have to work hard at it."

"And what might a veterinarian be?"

"An animal doctor — someone who takes care of people's pets when they're sick. The pets, that is, not the people."

"A noble occupation," approved Lung Wang. "Well, what's on for this afternoon?"

"Science class, and math — I hate that, it's so boring — and art, and music."

"Hmm! No instruction on the gods and spirits, I see, or *feng shui* — "

"*Feng shui?*"

"The magical powers that lie in the earth, and move through it like rivers — I can't believe you've never even heard of *feng shui!* It used to be that no self-respecting person in China would build a house without consulting a *feng shui* expert first — to make certain it was properly positioned for the earth-magic, you know. Don't worry, I've checked over your home — we dragons know all about *feng shui* — and I assure you it is most auspiciously located." ·

"Well, we haven't got any magic classes at this school," said Ai Lien. "No one here believes in magic at all."

"They couldn't, come to think of it," said Lung Wang, lifting his head like a dog sniffing the air. "Right now the magic-currents are telling me that that school of yours is most disastrously situated."

"Is it really?" asked Ai Lien. "Well, that explains a — "

"Who're you talking to?" said a voice behind her.

Ai Lien turned with a gasp. It was Jake! He advanced toward her, and she backed away. "Leave me alone!"

"This is my place now," Jake informed her, waving a hand at the woods. "Me 'n' my buddies are goin' to hang out here from now on. We're throwing you out."

"You never cared about this place before!" she cried furiously. "You're only doing this to be mean!" She looked around her quickly: the teacher on schoolyard duty was far away at the other end of the soccer field. She turned to leave the wood.

And then suddenly other figures appeared out of the trees: Jeff and Danny and the other boys who hung around with Jake; and Patti and Sue and Mei, all the ones who laughed with Jake in class. They moved forward together, making a circle around her so she couldn't get away.

"Hey you guys — Alien talks to herself!" Jake shouted. They all began to snicker.

"Go away!" Ai Lien cried. "Leave me alone!"

"Or maybe she isn't talking to herself!" Jake laughed. "Maybe she's talking to her little pet dragon!"

Ai Lien went pale. "What do you know about that?"

"Hah! She admits it!" Jake roared. He took another step toward her. "Your mom was talking to Mei's mom, and she told her all about it. A pretend-friend! What a baby!" He laughed and the others joined in. "Where's your dragon friend, Alien? Show us your pet dragon!"

Ai Lien backed away. She was beginning to be frightened, not so much for her own sake as for Lung Wang's. She could feel the tiny dragon crouching down at the very bottom of her pocket, trying not to be noticed. She put her hand in her pocket, touching him protectively.

Immediately she wished she hadn't, because at once Jake pounced. "What's in your pocket?" he demanded.

Ai Lien snatched her hand away. "Nothing!"

"It's not nothing, you're hiding something in there!" Jake said, striding forward. "I wanna know what it is." Whatever it was, he could see by her face that it was very important to her. Something he could take from her, something he could break or spoil.

He grabbed her by the arm, and all the boys followed his lead. The girls hung around tittering; Patti reached out and pulled Ai Lien's hair hard.

"Stop it, stop it!" she shouted, close to tears between her fury and her fear for Lung Wang. "I'll tell the teacher!"

"Go ahead, tell the teacher!" sneered Jake. "But let's see what's in your pocket first!"

She kicked and screamed, but it was no use. Jake plunged his hand into her pocket. Ai Lien turned her head; she couldn't bear to look.

All of a sudden there was a terrible yell from Jake, and the hands holding Ai Lien all let go at once. She stared in astonishment: Jake was dancing about wildly, howling with fear. Wrapped around his forearm was an enormous black-and-yellow garter snake, its forked tongue flicking at his face.

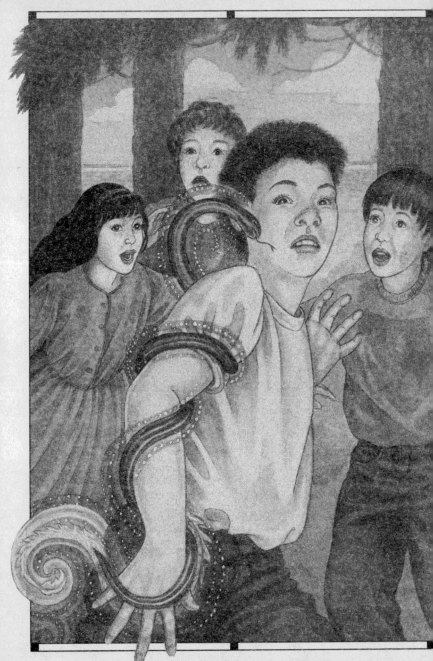

*Wrapped around his forearm was an enormous
black-and-yellow garter snake . . .*

"Get it off me, get it off me!" Jake yelped. He waved his arm frantically, and the snake dropped to the ground. It reared up hissing, then glided forward. With an assortment of shrieks and shouts the boys and girls jumped back out of the angry reptile's way.

Ai Lien laughed weakly. Of course it was only Lung Wang in another of his remarkable disguises. How clever of him to turn himself into a snake! She went over to him and picked him up carefully, slipping him back into her pocket. "There now — you're safe," she said.

A sudden silence fell. She glanced up to see everyone staring at her in open-mouthed amazement. Ai Lien looked them over, wondering how on earth she could ever have been afraid of them. Then she marched right past them. They hastily made room for her.

"It's only a *snake*," she said contemptuously as she strode by.

It was a supreme moment for her.

Chapter eight

Lung Wang to the Rescue

As the school year drew to a close, Ai Lien found to her surprise that Jake stayed away from her, and so did his followers.

In fact, Jake seemed to have fewer followers than before, while some of the kids were being friendlier toward Ai Lien. As Jeff said, you just *had* to admire a girl who carried live snakes around in her pocket. But even though he kept away from her, Ai Lien could feel Jake's eyes on her in class and in the schoolyard. She knew he had to be plotting revenge.

But Ai Lien pushed all thoughts of Jake from her mind once school ended. She never saw him, and in the fun of summer vacation she soon forgot about him.

grass and gazing up at the blue, blue sky. It only rained when Lung Wang allowed it to, and he arranged for it to happen only at night so it wouldn't spoil their plans.

They revelled in the lazy summer days, in all their sights and sounds and tastes and smells: the fragrance of newly mown grass, the songs of the birds and crickets, the sight of other children playing and shouting in the gardens all around, and the wonderful sweet taste of the popsicles that Mrs. Feng made for them out of frozen red bean soup, which always seemed to Ai Lien like the taste of Summer itself. Ai Lien thought that these things were somehow better than they had ever been before, now that she had someone to share them with.

Each day of that magical summer was like a bead in a beautiful long necklace, part of the whole yet special in its own way. On the weekends, Mr. and Mrs. Feng would take them to interesting places. They went to Ontario Place for the Canada Day fireworks. Watching the beautiful bursting shapes of gold, green, scarlet and purple, and hearing the delighted *ohhs* and *aahs* of the crowds, Ai Lien felt very proud to think that *her* ancestors had invented fireworks. They also visited the zoo and the museum. It proved difficult to get Lung Wang out of the museum's famous Chinese rooms, where he seemed inclined to spend the whole day admiring the ceramic dragons. He told Ai Lien the names of all the gods and goddesses whose statues stood in the big silent chambers, looking wise and solemn and very ancient. Mr. Feng also took them to Centre Island to watch the Dragon Boat Races, which were based on the ancient Chinese festival and were a lot of fun to watch: teams of people in boats with carved dragons' heads, all rowing like mad across the water while crowds cheered them on from the shores of the island.

Near the end of August there was a special event in High Park. It was called Children's Day, and there were to be games of all kinds, including a scavenger hunt. "I will take the day off work," Mrs. Feng told Ai Lien, "and take you over to High Park for the fun — and Wang too, if he'd like to come. It will be good for you both to be with other children your age."

Ai Lien didn't much want to go, but when she told Lung Wang about it he was interested. "It would be a good opportunity for me to learn more about humans," he told her. Ai Lien thought that it would probably be fun for him, too. Lung Wang had not played very many games in his short life, she reflected. And so when the day came Ai Lien went with her mother to High Park, and they took Lung Wang with them. The dragon had slipped out of the house earlier and joined them on the sidewalk in his human shape, pretending that he had come from another house nearby.

"I'm glad to see Ai Lien has a friend," Mrs. Feng told him. "It's too bad you aren't staying here, Wang. How long will you be here in Canada?"

"Oh, for a while yet," replied Lung Wang vaguely.

"I'm surprised your parents would let you go off to another country by yourself when you're so young," Mrs. Feng continued. "I suppose you're staying with relatives."

"No—o," he said with a glance at Ai Lien, "I am currently residing at the house of a friend."

"That's very nice for you."

"Oh, I assure you it is a most satisfactory arrangement," Lung Wang replied.

"What a funny little boy he is," said Mrs. Feng to Ai Lien when Lung Wang had run ahead to look at the swans in Grenadier Pond. "He uses such long words!"

"He hasn't been speaking English for very long," Ai Lien improvised. "I don't think he knows how Canadian people talk yet."

"Yes — he sounds a bit as though he were reading from a book, doesn't he?" mused her mother.

Ai Lien quite enjoyed the activities, after all. There were a lot of familiar faces from her school there, including Jake Bradley, who was oddly silent, looking away if she glanced in his direction. They were all very curious about Lung Wang. "His name's Wang, and he's a visitor from China," she explained, over and over.

"Where in China?" Mei asked.

"I come from the bank of the Yangtze River," Lung Wang told her.

Mei looked at him. "Would you like to be my partner in the three-legged race?" she asked.

"Impossible, I'm afraid," he told her. "I have already promised to accompany Ai Lien. She is my friend, you see."

Lung Wang enjoyed himself enormously "researching human customs" as he called it. He and Ai Lien won the egg-tossing competition and were each presented with a bright plastic yo-yo. She had to explain to him what it was.

"A curious artifact," he said, holding it up and studying it closely. "I'll keep it and take it back to my father's court when I go. I'm sure they will find it intriguing."

The last event of the day was a scavenger hunt. Ai Lien had never gone on one before and she found it quite exciting. The children were divided into teams, each with an adult in charge, and each team had to beat the others in finding a long list of items. Oddly, Jake ended up choosing Ai Lien's team. "Maybe he's trying to be friends," she remarked to Lung Wang. But Jake, she noticed, still avoided her eye and made no effort to speak to her.

After an hour's searching their team had found everything except one item, a live earthworm. Their team leader suggested they give up looking for the worm and go back to the central meeting place.

"Shall I turn myself into one?" Lung Wang whispered in Ai Lien's ear. He was all excited by the hunt, and taking it more seriously than anyone else.

"I guess it wouldn't be fair to the other teams," Ai Lien whispered back regretfully. "Ours is the only team with a dragon on it."

"Then I'll see if I can find a worm somewhere," he said, "I refuse to give up — " And before she could stop him he had slipped off into the woods, away from the rest of the group.

She ran after him. "Wang?" she called, softly. "Lung Wang, I don't think we should wander away from the rest of the group." But there was no reply, and she hurried on through the trees.

A little distance ahead, the woods sloped into a ravine with a stream at the bottom. At the far end she could see Lung Wang walking along the bank, poking at the mud with a stick in the effort to find an earthworm. Ai Lien started to climb down the side of the ravine.

"Hah! I've got you now!" said Jake's voice triumphantly, behind her. "Alien!"

Ai Lien whirled around. He was standing not far away, an ugly, sneering expression on his face. She looked frantically up the ravine, but Lung Wang had vanished from sight. "Wang?" she called, uncertainly.

"You've wrecked everything for me," growled Jake, walking toward her. "You made me look bad in front of the others. You got me in trouble with everyone — "

"It was your own fault!" Ai Lien burst out. "You were being mean to me — " And then she stopped, frightened, because Jake's face looked so strange, so pale with anger that his freckles stood out.

Jake laughed a horrible laugh. "I'll show you! There's no teacher here now!"

Ai Lien thought quickly. The pockets of her shorts were not big enough to hold a garter snake, so she couldn't threaten him with that. Everyone else was too far away to hear her if she yelled. The woods were terribly still and quiet as Jake advanced toward her.

"May I ask what exactly is going on here?" came Lung Wang's voice from off to the right.

Jake whirled in his turn as the small Chinese boy

stepped out of the bushes and strolled toward them unconcernedly, his hands in his pockets. Ai Lien's heart leaped.

"Get outta here," Jake snarled.

"Gladly," said Lung Wang. "Come along, Ai Lien, let's leave this unpleasant personage to himself, shall we?"

"Oh, no, you don't!" Jake shouted. "Ai Lien stays here. Now *you* get lost, or I'll punch your face."

"Ugly and uncouth barbarian," retorted Lung Wang. "I'd like to see you try."

Ai Lien looked around her desperately. She could see that Jake was in a dangerous mood, and meant to fight with Lung Wang. Of course the dragon-boy had powers that Jake didn't have, but how could he use magic without giving himself away? She knew she should go and fetch the team leader to stop the fight, but she didn't like to leave Lung Wang.

"Go on, Ai Lien," Lung Wang said to her. "I'll be all right! I require no assistance."

"Big words, big words," sneered Jake. "Let's see you *do* something, you sissy."

"I don't know what a 'sissy' might be," answered Lung Wang, his dark eyes beginning to glint dangerously, "but as for doing something, I'd be delighted to oblige. I could strike you with ten thousand lightning bolts if I chose —

but I won't," he added, seeing Ai Lien's shocked expression. "I will not fight with a mere mortal. It wouldn't be fair."

"Who're you calling a mortal?" snapped Jake, clenching his fists. He had no idea what the word meant, but Lung Wang's tone showed it was no compliment. "Are you trying to insult me?"

"Trying? I appear to be succeeding," was Lung's disdainful reply.

Jake flung himself at the other boy in a rage, hitting him on the nose. Lung Wang stumbled and sat down abruptly on the ground. Triumphantly, Jake turned his back on Lung Wang and advanced toward Ai Lien with a menacing smirk.

Ai Lien backed away, her fists clenched in anger. "You bully!" she cried, her voice trembling, "He's smaller than you, it's not fair!" As Jake forced her up the side of the ravine she saw, over his shoulder, Lung Wang get to his feet, rubbing his nose. Pain was a new sensation to him, and it was clear he didn't much care for it.

"I may be smaller now," she heard him say, "but I won't be for long." Even as he spoke, the figure of the Chinese boy began to change, growing larger and longer and sprouting red and golden scales.

"No, don't," Ai Lien screamed, "it's not worth it!"

Jake, his back to Lung Wang, was exultant. Worth it? He had been waiting all year for this! At last he had succeeded in making her terrified of him! He raised his fist. "So much for your sissy friend!" he gloated, "and so much for you!"

"No, Jake, don't!" cried Ai Lien. "You don't understand! He's not a boy at all — he's a dragon, and you've made him very angry!"

"Liar!" Jake answered scornfully. "You and your dragons! You think you can fool me that easily?"

The dragon was crawling toward Jake, his green eyes blazing.

"I tell you he's a dragon!" shouted Ai Lien, her back to a tree, now. "Jake, stop — *he's right behind you!*"

"I'm not gonna fall for that old trick!" Jake yelled back. "Stupid! Everyone knows there's no such thing as — "

A low, deep growl came rumbling from behind him. Jake froze. Slowly, he turned around.

And found himself staring full into a pair of giant green eyes, in a red-and-golden scaly face, all horns and teeth.

Jake stood absolutely motionless for one second. Then with a scream he took off running. He tore through the trees bawling: "Help, help! Dragon — there's a dragon in the woods!"

He fled the woods and ran wildly through the park,

Jake stood absolutely motionless for one second.

yelling at the top of his voice as he went. "A dragon —
I saw a dragon! Help, help!"

He blundered into the rest of the scavenger hunt team,
still shouting. They all gave him withering looks.
"Gimme a break, Jake!" said Mei. "There are no such
things as dragons, you've said so yourself!"

"But I saw it, I tell you!" Jake panted in fright.

"You're nuts," said Jeff. "Dragon, my foot!"

"Maybe he saw another garter snake!" suggested Ben.
And they all started giggling.

"But I *did* see a dragon," Jake wailed as they all turned
away. "You've got to believe me!"

But no one did.

Chapter nine

The Dragon Palace

Summer drew to a close. The days became shorter and more golden, the nights cooler. The trees were still green, but patches of leaves here and there were turning red or yellow. Sometimes in the night flocks of Canada geese would fly over the house, calling out in their high, wild voices. "Summer is ending," they seemed to be saying. "Winter is on its way."

Lung Wang seemed restless, too. In his dragon shape he was now enormous, almost as tall as the elephants at the zoo and quite a lot longer. So he had to either shrink himself or take another shape in order to live inside the house. Sometimes he went out at night when everyone was asleep, and returning to his own huge size

116

he would lie curled up in the little garden, gazing wistfully at the sky. But when the nights grew chillier he stopped going out. He became moody and fretful, poring endlessly over Mr. Feng's books on China, staring by the hour at pictures of tall mountains and winding rivers. Ai Lien sympathized with him, knowing how confined he must feel.

She had been back at school for a week now, and had found that everyone was much nicer to her. In fact some of them even wanted to be friends: Mei had started sitting next to her in class, and the other girls called her over as they stood about and talked together at recess. She even managed to talk some of them into playing a game of tag one day, "for old time's sake." They enjoyed it enormously. A lot of the kids in her class, she realized, had only stayed away from her because they were afraid of Jake. Now that Ai Lien had shown him up as a coward, no one was afraid of him any longer.

Jake himself she hardly ever saw at all, as he was in another Grade Six class. If they did meet in the hallway or on the playground he always looked away — afraid, perhaps, that she would call on her dragon friend again.

Ai Lien was rather sorry for him. The kids who had been in the park on Children's Day never let Jake forget what a fool he had been. They sneered and called him names, but Ai Lien never joined in. "Jake and I," she explained to Lung Wang, "are the only people in the world today who know that dragons are real."

Ai Lien's tenth birthday was approaching fast. It was Lung Wang's birthday too, as he had been hatched before midnight on the same day; he would be one year old. She liked the idea of sharing a birthday with him, and, when the day came at last, she asked Grandmother to take her down to Dundas Street after school so she could buy a present for her friend. She still had her lucky money from New Year's, which she had been saving up for something special. After some searching she found a little carved wooden dragon in one of the gift stores. Ai Lien thought it looked rather like Lung Wang himself. She was sure he would love it.

Her mother came home early on the day of Ai Lien's birthday, so there was no after-school visit with Lung Wang. She decided to give him his present after dinner. Her mother's present to her was a beautiful new special-occasion dress, all white and lacy with a skirt that reached to the floor. She tried it on, and when her father saw her in it he smiled and sighed.

"How grown up you're getting, Ai Lien!" he said, a bit regretfully.

"I know," Ai Lien said. "I'm beginning to feel rather

old." He burst out laughing at that — grown-ups, she thought, laughed for the oddest reasons.

After dinner she rushed up to her room. Lung Wang was lying coiled up on her bed, having shrunk himself to a manageable size. He looked rather gloomy.

"Happy birthday, Lung Wang!" she cried, holding out the wooden dragon. "Here's your present!"

He brightened a little at the sight of it, and took it carefully in his claw. "Whoever made this knows all about dragons, even if he never saw one," he declared, pleased. Then he sighed. "And I've got you nothing — "

"I wouldn't expect you to," she said hurriedly. "After all, you haven't got any money. Anyway, I've had lots of nice presents — though nothing as nice as the one I got last year."

"What's that?" he asked absently.

"You!" she laughed.

But he didn't join in her laughter. "What's the matter?" she asked, sitting down beside him. "You look sort of sad."

"I am sad," he said. "And happy too. Do you notice something different about me?"

She looked at him carefully. "Yes — there's a sort of bump on your head, like an extra large scale . . . oh." Her voice trailed away and she fell silent.

"Yes, it's my *chi'h muh*," Lung Wang told her. "Ai Lien, I'm ready to fly now. It's time for me to go home."

"Oh," she said again. Her heart sank. "I'm sorry — I mean, I'm glad you're going back to your family. But I'm sorry you're leaving — I'll miss you so much." And then she found she couldn't say any more. Her throat felt strangely tight.

"I'm sorry, too," he said. "It has been a — a most felicitous arrangement."

"What does 'felicitous' mean?" she asked with a sniff.

"It means I'm very glad I met you." He rested his scaly chin on her shoulder for a moment. Then suddenly he gave an exclamation.

"What is it?" she asked.

"I've just had an idea," he said. "Ai Lien, why don't you come to China with me?"

She stared at him, wide-eyed. "Oh!" she cried. "But — Mummy and Daddy would never let me — "

"I don't mean to stay," he explained quickly. "Just for a visit. We dragons can fly faster than airplanes — faster than the wind. I could fly you there and back again before anyone even missed you!"

A sudden longing filled Ai Lien — longing to see the marvellous palace of the Dragon King, which she had heard so much about but never dreamed of seeing for herself. Her sadness disappeared behind her excitement. "Yes — let's!" she cried joyfully. "After all — Daddy has always said he wants me to see China!"

They decided to go around midnight, after the grown-ups had gone to sleep: Lung Wang would slip outdoors and wait for her in the garden, taking his own shape as soon as the lights in the neighbouring houses were all out. The time seemed to pass very slowly: it felt to Ai Lien like an age before her parents came upstairs and settled down in their room to sleep. At last the hands on Ai Lien's little clock reached twelve. Lung Wang was waiting for her down in the garden. She jumped out of bed, listened cautiously for any sound from her parents' room, and then ran to her closet. What should she wear for the trip? Nothing she had seemed grand enough for a Dragon King's palace. Then her eye fell upon the Chinese robe she'd been given last year. It had dragons embroidered on it, and there were the little slippers that matched. Quickly she pulled off her nightie and threw on the robe. The house was dark and very still when Ai Lien finally crept downstairs and into the garden.

"Ah, there you are!" said Lung Wang. He had returned to his own enormous size, so that he had to lie down flat for Ai Lien to scramble up onto his back. In one claw he clutched his magic pearl, which was glowing softly.

In the other were his present from Ai Lien and the yo-yo he'd won in the race. He passed these to her. "Just hold onto these things for me, would you? That's it! Now — are you ready?"

Ai Lien nodded, her eyes sparkling with excitement. "Ready!" she said.

Lung Wang lifted the pearl high and said something in Chinese. The pearl glowed brightly, and there was an answering glimmer from the *chi'h muh* on Lung Wang's head. And then they were rising into the air.

Ai Lien had flown once before, in an airplane with her parents. But this was different. She could feel the wind blowing in her face, fresh and cool, and there was no noisy engine to drown out the sounds of the night. She could see all sorts of things from this height, things that were usually hidden: the neighbours' gardens all came into view, with their vegetable patches and flower beds, and she was fascinated to see what large shadows the trees and houses cast under the moon. Every evening she'd watched the darkness steal across the garden as the sun slowly set, but somehow she'd never *thought* of that darkness as being the shadow of the house next door. Now she could clearly see that that was what it was. And how very tiny everything seemed: the trees and houses looked just like those in the toy village she'd played with when she was small.

She looked to the south, and saw all the things that the houses had always blocked from her view when she was down on the ground: the big, lit-up buildings downtown, the CN Tower with its lights flashing, and the lake beyond, all blue and dim with here and there the small faint light of a boat on it. Suddenly there was a noise of rushing wings and a loud *honk-honk*, and a whole flock of Canada geese flew past, the small dark eyes above their white cheeks astonished as they stared at the girl and dragon. They came so close that Ai Lien could almost have touched the tip of the nearest goose's moon-silvered wing. She laughed out loud in sheer delight.

Then they turned westward in a great sweeping curve and Lung Wang shouted: "Hold on tight! I'm going to fly like the wind," and she clung to the big upright scales on his back as the whole world turned into a rushing darkness full of noise.

"Ai Lien! Ai Lien!"

Lung Wang was calling out to her, his voice filled with excitement. "We're here, we're here! We're in China!"

Ai Lien blinked. There was light all around her, yellow-white and brilliant.

"Gosh — it's *sunlight!*" she gasped. "Did I fall asleep?" She didn't think she had.

"No, you didn't." Lung Wang turned his head around to look at her, his green eyes twinkling. "We dragons fly by magic, so it takes us hardly any time at all to get from one place to another."

"But why is it daylight?"

"Remember what you learned in school? The earth turns and the sun's light strikes different parts of it at different times, so it's midday in China when it's midnight in Canada, and so on. We're in a different time zone now."

"Of course," said Ai Lien, remembering. She sat up straight and looked around her.

They were flying over a land of green rolling hills. Far below them a great river wound through a steep-sided gorge. "The Yangtze," Lung Wang told her. "I'd better get underwater quickly, or someone will see me."

As a matter of fact only one person saw Lung Wang and Ai Lien, a little girl of six named Jin. She ran at once to her mother, who was pinning up clothes on a line. "Mama, Mama, I saw a dragon!"

"That's nice, dear," said her mother, hanging up a shirt.

"It was a big dragon," said Jin. "All red and gold. There

was a girl on its back, she was riding it. It looked like fun — I wish I had a dragon."

"Mmm," her mother said.

Meanwhile Lung Wang and Ai Lien were skimming along just above the surface of the river. "Won't we get all wet?" she asked nervously, but Lung explained that his magic would keep them dry. Then he dived.

One moment they were in bright sunshine; the next instant they were underwater, the river's depths all green and murky around them. Ai Lien found to her relief that she could breathe with perfect ease: it must be the magic. Fish swam past them in silvery schools, and once a *beiji*, the little river-dolphin of the Yangtze, glided up to them, stared with his tiny dark eye and made clicking sounds.

"He was talking, wasn't he?" exclaimed Ai Lien delightedly as the dolphin swam on.

"Yes — he said, 'Greetings, Prince. All the river rejoices at your return!' Nice creatures, the river-dolphins: they've become rather scarce nowadays, owing to all the pollution."

On and on they swam through the green depths. Suddenly the dragon gave a cry. "Look — there's the palace! Just as Mother and Father described it to me!"

She looked down into the green darkness below, and

saw to her amazement and delight the shapes of towers rising up out of the depths. They had beautiful carved roofs like pagodas, and warm light poured out of their windows. Tiny fish swarmed around these, attracted like insects to the light.

And then Lung Wang was walking on the river bottom, toward a great set of carved doors. On either side were enormous eels, like guard dogs. They uncoiled themselves at once, toothy jaws agape, but when they saw Lung Wang they bowed their huge heads and let him pass. The dragon went up to the doors and pushed them open.

Light flooded out in golden beams, lighting up the river's rocky bed. Lung Wang strode into the palace with Ai Lien on his back. Glancing behind her, she saw that the water did not come in through the doors: some kind of magic kept it out. It formed a kind of watery wall, like the rippling, reflecting surface of a swimming pool turned on end. Then she turned to look ahead of her, and forgot everything else in her awe at the scene before her.

She and Lung Wang stood in a great hall, bigger than the gymnasium at school, grander than the dining hall of the Golden Dragon Restaurant. Golden pillars with carved dragons coiled around them stood to either side, and the walls were red, patterned with gold, while enormous tasseled lanterns hung from the ceiling. At the far end of the hall was a platform with two thrones on it, and in the thrones were two figures dressed in splendid robes. One was a lady beautiful as a porcelain figurine. Her dark hair was piled high on her head, and her gown was green and peacock blue. Next to her sat a tall man robed in red whose black beard fell to his waist. Ai Lien knew at once that these were the rulers of the river, the Dragon Queen and King.

The great hall was filled with people — if "people" was the right word, for none of them was human, though some had taken human shapes. There were dragons of all colours and sizes: water-dragons like Lung Wang, and dragons of the air, the earth and the heavens. There were tall, majestic-looking men and women who Lung Wang told her were spirits of the earth, the waters and the sky. There was the *chi'lin*, one of the messengers of Heaven: a beautiful, graceful animal with the body and slender legs of a deer, a dragonlike head and a single stag's horn growing between his eyes. There were two large brightly coloured birds with heads like pheasants' and peacock plumes on their tail feathers: the *feng-hwang* birds. Near them was a huge tortoise, bigger than the ones Ai Lien had seen in pictures of the Galapagos

Islands, with a wise, wizened face. And beside the dais stood a hare, so big and handsome and with such a lovely silvery shine to his white fur that he could only be the Hare of the Moon himself.

Ai Lien slipped off Lung's back and walked beside him up the centre of the hall. All the spirits and creatures watched as the dragon and the little girl went up to the two thrones on their platform and bowed low. And although they had made themselves look human — "So you won't feel shy, I think," whispered Lung Wang — still Ai Lien could not look at the King and Queen directly, and stood with her eyes lowered, gazing at the floor.

But the Dragon Queen spoke in such a gentle musical voice that Ai Lien found she *was* able to look up, into the beautiful face. "Lung Wang, our son! We are overjoyed to have you back with us at last! You were seen approaching the coast, and so we have all assembled in your honour."

"Mother!" Ai Lien turned to see that Lung Wang had once more taken the shape of a little boy. He ran up to the Queen, who kissed him and held him close, and an attendant came forward and put a glorious golden robe over Lung Wang's shoulders.

Then he turned to the King. "Father."

Ai Lien slipped off Lung Wang's back and walked beside him
up the centre of the hall.

"My son," said the King, in a deep, powerful voice. "Welcome back to my court!"

"I'm sorry!" Ai Lien burst out. "I'm so sorry Daddy took Lung Wang away from you. He didn't mean to — he thought the egg was a stone . . . " Her voice trailed away as the assembled creatures looked at her and she dropped her gaze again.

But the Queen came down from her throne, her silken robes rustling, and very gently put her smooth, pale hand under Ai Lien's chin, making her look up. "My dear child, of course we understand that," she said softly. "It was an accident, no more; and now we have our dear son back, so there is no harm done. But come, let Lung Wang himself tell of his adventures in the world of human beings."

The King clapped his hands, and cushions were brought for Lung Wang and Ai Lien to sit on. And Lung Wang told them all about growing up in a faraway land, and of his friendship with Ai Lien. Then he asked her for the yo-yo, and began to do tricks with it, to the delight of the court. After that he showed the wooden dragon to his parents.

The Dragon King beamed when he saw the little carving.

"Truly, your people have not forgotten us after all,

Ai Lien," he said. "They may be living in a far-off land, setting aside the old customs for new, foreign ways, but they have not forgotten the old magic. Perhaps some day dragons and humans will be friends again. You and Lung Wang have shown that it is possible."

"Oh, Lung Wang has been such a good friend to me!" she cried, forgetting her shyness, and proceeded to tell the court all about the great fight with Jake, while Lung Wang sat by looking modest.

"From what we have heard," said the Queen, "you have been as good a friend to Lung Wang. You gave him a home, fed him and kept him safe. We can never repay you."

"Yes we can!" said Lung Wang suddenly. He turned to Ai Lien. "Stay with us!" he pleaded. "Be part of our family! We'll make you a princess, and you could live here in the palace with us."

"Yes!" the dragons chorused. "Please stay! We never see humans any more, and you are so interesting!"

Just then there came a loud "Ahem!" from the back of the hall, and a figure walked forward, toward the royal thrones. It was a short, stout little man, with a bearded face that looked as though it could be merry, though just now it was serious.

"Oh, my!" said Ai Lien. "It's the Kitchen God!" He

looked exactly as she had always imagined him.

The Kitchen God went up to the King and Queen and bowed slightly, then looked around at the people in the hall. "You seem to forget," he said quietly, "that Ai Lien has a family of her own."

"Of course," said Ai Lien. "Mummy and Daddy and Grandmother would be so unhappy if I didn't go home — just as unhappy as you all were when Lung Wang was taken away."

Lung Wang's face fell. "You're right," he said sadly.

"Certainly the Kitchen God is right," said the Dragon Queen. "Ai Lien must return to her own people."

Lung Wang looked at Ai Lien. "So — this really is goodbye then."

She nodded, unable to speak.

"Perhaps you can come visit us some day," he suggested hopefully.

"That won't be for years and years," she replied, blinking her tears back. "And it won't be the same as having you at home with me. Lung Wang, I'll miss you so much!"

Lung Wang seemed to be having trouble speaking. "Me too," he managed to say at last, in a low voice. Tears filled Ai Lien's eyes and she looked away for several moments, trying hard not to cry.

"Ai Lien — are you ready to go back now?" asked the soft voice of the Dragon Queen at last. Ai Lien turned, to see that Lung Wang and his parents had all taken their real, dragon shapes. The King and Queen were red and gold, like their son, though the Queen's eyes were blue as sapphires and the King's as red as rubies. They were both so big, so proud and so beautiful, that she was overwhelmed at the sight of them and couldn't speak.

"Let *me* take her home," volunteered Lung Wang in a low voice, "since I know the way." The Dragon King nodded his great head.

Lung Wang knelt down so that she could climb onto his back and they returned to the great doors together, moving slowly past the dragons, the *chi'lin,* the *feng-hwang* and the Moon Hare.

"Come back to us some day!" the dragons called after her in voices like trumpets.

"Do not forget the magic!" came the sweet bell-like voice of the *chi'lin*. "Keep it in your heart always!"

"We will always remember you," sang the *feng-hwang*.

"Do not forget us!" they all cried together.

And then the doors were opening, and Ai Lien and Lung Wang were rising up through the river, to the sun above.

It was nearly dawn when they returned to the little house in Toronto. Ai Lien climbed very slowly off Lung Wang's back, and then flung her arms as far as they would go around his huge neck. He lowered his chin to her shoulder and they stood that way for a long time.

At last Ai Lien released her hold and stepped back. "Goodbye," she whispered.

"Goodbye, Ai Lien," he answered. "For now."

And then he turned and soared up into the air, the pearl glowing in his claw. High overhead, he circled above the house three times, as though he were blessing it. Then he flew away westward, toward China and the Dragon Palace. For some time Ai Lien could still see the light of the pearl, shining through the grey dawn like a star.

Chapter ten

The Magic

Ai Lien slept in late that morning, and woke up feeling gloomy. It took her a moment to realize why. Then she remembered, and sighed out loud.

Lung Wang was gone! He had returned home at last, as he'd always said he would. How empty her little room looked — how dull everything seemed! She got up and dressed herself slowly. At least today was Saturday and there was no school: she doubted she could have got through a whole day pretending nothing was wrong.

Her parents did not know what to make of her. "You're very quiet, Ai Lien," her mother said with concern. "You're not feeling sick, are you?"

"No," answered Ai Lien listlessly.

"Why don't you go out and play with Wang?" suggested her father cheerfully.

"He's gone. He flew back to China," Ai Lien told them.

"Oh — and you're missing him," exclaimed Mr. Feng. "Poor Ai Lien!"

"You'll find another friend," Mrs. Feng promised her. "Maybe at school."

"Not like him." Ai Lien felt tears coming close. She had lots of friends at school now. But how could any ordinary human friend compare to Lung Wang?

"Perhaps she'd like to have a dog," said her father. "Like that little Pekingese she looked after. Would you like a dog of your own, Ai Lien?" he asked, taking her by the hand.

"That would be . . . nice," she replied, trying hard to sound enthusiastic. How could any ordinary dog compare to Lung Wang?

After dinner that evening Ai Lien went out into the garden. It was only about seven-thirty, but already the sky was growing dark. The air was cool. She stood looking up at the sky, remembering how Lung Wang had flown away through it the night before. Sighing deeply, she turned to go back into the house.

Something on the ground glittered, catching her eye. She went over and picked it up, curious. It was a small green gem — its colour reminded her of the depths of the Yangtze River. Folded underneath it was a note. She snatched this up eagerly, for she recognized the large sprawling handwriting on it as Lung Wang's. She'd been teaching him to write just before he left.

Dear Ai Lien:

Here is your belated birthday present. My mother is sending it by the fastest dragon at court — one who flies so fast that no one can even see him! This jewel is a magic dragon-gem that will bring you good luck.

Think of me often! I'll be thinking of you. The Dragon Palace is a wonderful place, but I'll like it even better when you come one day to stay!

Your friend, Lung Wang

Ai Lien stood for a moment, looking up at the sky. She could almost hear Lung Wang's voice, and the voices of the other magical creatures in the faraway palace: *Keep the magic in your heart always. . . do not forget us!*

The stars were coming out in the evening sky: they looked to her like splendidly robed people, gazing down on her with wise and kindly eyes. She looked up at the moon, and saw a white hare who twitched his nose at her in a friendly way. Dragons leaped and danced on the

She could almost hear Lung Wang's voice, and the voices of the other magical creatures. . .

wind, among the silvery clouds. She felt as though she were surrounded by loving friends, and knew that, with the magic in her heart, she would never be alone again.

"I won't forget!" she called out to the sky, to the moon and to the stars. "I won't forget!"

Then she turned and went back into the house.

Alison Baird has been writing since she was very young, and she published her first poems when she was twelve years old! *The Dragon's Egg* was her first published book, and it went on to be a Regional Winner of the Silver Birch Award. She is also the author of several novels for teens and adults.

Alison's grandparents lived in China for a time, and her father was born there. One of the mementos the family brought back to Canada was a vase patterned with dragons, which fascinated Alison when she was a child. Perhaps the dragons enchanted her as well, because she loves to write about magic!

Alison currently lives in Oakville, Ontario.

Illustrator Frances Tyrrell likes to paint magic into the everyday world. She is known for her exquisite fairy paintings, and has illustrated several books, including *Woodland Christmas: Twelve Days of Christmas in the North Woods* and *The Huron Carol*, which were both nominated for the Governor General's Award.

Frances lives in Oakville, Ontario.